Terrakonans

By:

Llewellyn Burgess

DEDICATION

Dedicated to the Lilies of Aethersong Free Company on Aegis Server and especially their leader Ophelia Laoghaire.   May your tea times always remain inspirational.

CONTENTS

ACKNOWLEDGMENTS

Special thanks to Reiko Asahiru for doing the cover art.

And Marlinda Davis for Beta Reading

Chapter 1

It was a quiet day, just like any other. Well quiet, meaning peaceful. The birds were singing, the brook was babbling, and the blacksmith was hammering away at his latest orders. The smell of freshly baked goods in the air was giving way to the stench of manure as the sun was finally starting to clear the hilltops and shone down into the valley.

A woman opened her eyes, looking up at the sky in a field of flowers just outside of her hometown. Her long, amber hair seemed like an endless contrast alongside her ebony eyes. The violent sound of multiple wings flapping together jolted her from her spot. A murder of crows. Without disrupting her poise, she turned her head to see what all the noise was about.

Her eyes lifted as they traced their commotion. She could barely make out that they were dancing about a pile of metal. Rising from her seated position, she brushed some stray grass from her dress as she silently moved towards the site her eyes couldn't seem to break from.

As she moved closer, it became apparent that the heap of metal was actually a suit of armour, or rather, what was left of it. What once was a symbol of protection lay before her in a hopeless heap, a pathetic representation of the prestige it once held.

The sharp edges were rounded into a giant mass of metal. The helmet, breastplate, leggings and sabatons had all amalgamated into one; the only non-rounded edge was three marks that diagonally crossed over the back of the armour. She found it odd that although the metal was melted, a clear indication of being exposed to high heat or *some* sort of reaction of high intensity, there were no burn marks to speak of. Yet the vegetation at the feet of the armour's body had been flattened. She approached the body carefully while glancing around her, keeping her ears perked up for any suspicious sound or movement.

As she drew closer to the body, she breathed in deep in an attempt to detect any scents that might give off clues to what was going on but there was none. With no reason to be alarmed, the woman reached out to touch the armour with her pointer finger. To her surprise, it was as cold as ice. Stretching her arm out more, she leaned forward until her whole hand lay tenderly on the armour. It was still ice cold.

Brushing her fingers over the suit of armour, she moved her hand up towards the jagged opening, marvelling at its girth as her hand disappeared within its depths. Feeling around inside it, she discovered that the body of whoever was wearing it was still intact albeit the skin felt a little tight and there was no liquid.

Finding this odd, she withdrew her hand and started to get up. Right at that moment, she felt something grasp her waist, pulling her back down to the ground. Panic set in as she tried to get away while realising the hand extended from the corpse she was just examining. Her vision blurred as the ground and sky seemed to dance around her ultimately leading her to darkness.

....

She didn't know how long she had been unconscious for, but when she came to, the darkness of night cuddled her like an ebony blanket. A sharp pain ripped through her head as the bells chimed off in the distance. With each ring the bell made, her pain faded away, little by little and a faint green light cut through the dark like heaven's gates opening…but green…

"Where am I?" she softly muttered under her breath.

The bell chimed again bringing with it a painful jolt through her body that pounded in her head twice as much as the first time. It was all she could do to brace her head between both palms of her hands willing it to stop.

In doing so, she noticed a green glow coming from her left hand. The hue seemed to fade in sync with the resonating ringing of the bell. Bringing her arm down, she looked at the back of her hand and forearm. The outline of what she saw looked similar to scaly wings that ran the length of her forearm.

Suddenly out of nowhere, a voice echoed around her, "I'm sorry to have suddenly pulled you in like this". The light seemed to vibrate with the voice, amplifying its soft warm tone.

"This? Who are you?" Morrigan asked.

"Mmm," a slow, deep rumble permeated that area causing Morrigan to stumble. "My former vessel has fallen to unfortunate circumstances, and to prevent my presence from disappearing on Gerrin we had to transfer my mark from them to you." There was a brief pause before it continued, "however, most times the vessels are groomed and prepared for the transfer, but in your case, it was an emergency and we had to act quickly."

"A vessel?" Morrigan spoke with a high-pitched squeal, "for what? I don't understand!" she shrieked, embracing her head more tightly unsure if her headache was due to being unsure of what was going on or the light and voice.

"Why do you need a vessel to keep your presence on the planet?" Morrigan touched the green light permeating from her left wrist, pursing her lips tightly. At the same time, the light began to take shape, first contouring to a circular shape which then stretched to an oval. The top of the oval slithered forward like a snake enchanted by a snake charmer's spell to form a snout. The midseam of the back of the oval split, stretching backwards to spread into large, webbed wings. The front midseam and bottom split into four claws, the bottom claws spread wide as the glob took form, revealing the full form of a dragon, albeit a very hazy form and not fully solid.

"A-a-a D-d-dragon!" Morrigan stammered, eyes dilated. At that moment her feet didn't seem to be able to move fast enough to even make a big escape. Try as she might, the distance between herself and the newly formed dragon did not increase at all. Instead, it stayed the same and constant.

"Do not be afraid," the dragon's voice was warm and soothing, "for I am you and you are me." The dragon bent over until its snout was level with Morrigan. Morrigan closed her eyes tightly as she felt the heat from its snout blanket her face.

"Please don't kill me," she barely managed to speak, "I- I didn't do anything," she blurted as she burst into a puddle of tears, curling tightly into a ball.

"Open your eyes young one, I mean you no harm," the dragon said as it stood up tall on all four feet. Looking off into the distance briefly, the dragon continued, "As I said before, I am sorry for the sudden intervention, but if you really want to avoid dying, you are going to have to develop some form of trust with me."

Morrigan slowly opened her eyes, her body clenched as stiff as a statue, "I guess you haven't killed me yet," she started, "but why spare me?"

"I am you and you are me," the dragon repeated patiently. "When my previous vessel touched you, you became imbued with my energies." Motioning towards her hand the dragon continued, "That mark on your arm is a pact between you and I. Should you ever need my power or help you only need to ask and I will be instantly at your side, fighting for your cause. As our bond grows stronger, you shall be privy to more of the workings of us dragons."

"What should I call you?" Morrigan sniffed, relaxing her body a little.

"Verthandi," the dragon responded as its form began to fade away. "Your time in this dimension is up; your body has stabilised with the new surge of energy. I will never be far away, but I suggest you leave your town and head south."

"Why?" Morrigan demanded.

"That which killed my previous vessel will soon be after you. Unless you wish to endanger innocents, you should leave and go south. There you will find one who will better train you as a Terrakonans."

"Wait!" Morrigan yelled as the dragon's form dispersed. "Come back!" she screamed, trying to reach out and grasp Verthandi's essence. Instead of grabbing the essence, she was engulfed by a white cloud as her vision returned. When she could see again, she found herself looking up at the clear blue sky. Her breathing was laboured, and she put her hand on her heart as it felt like it was about to beat right out of her chest.

Looking around her, she saw that her pail and spade were still nearby, but the body had disappeared. The air was still, and the only noticeable sound around her was the beautiful melody of songbirds and the babbling brook flowing beside her.

"Was it all just a dream?" she thought aloud as she sat up. Turning her hands in front of her, Morrigan looked at her palms and then the back of her hands. She then felt a searing on her left shoulder and bent over in pain as she held the offending shoulder. She grimaced but did not scream out as she felt the burning sensation. For a few intense moments it rendered her helpless. Just as quickly as it ravaged her body, the pain subsided.

She moved her hand slowly as motion returned to her body, the smell of burnt flesh wafting up to her nostrils. Reaching up to her shoulder she ran her fingers gently over it. To her surprise, she felt some patches of raised flesh. She pulled down the nape of her dress to reveal what looked like a winged pattern branded on each shoulder. As the burnt smell dissipated, it turned a pale green. "What is happening?" she whispered with a shudder.

"Go South... You don't have much time..." she heard a whisper materialise out of nowhere.

"How?" she shivered, but her thought was broken as she heard someone hail out to her.

"Morrigan! Morrigan!" a man's voice was calling out to her.

Morrigan scrambled to her feet but faced her mark shoulder away from the approaching man. "Hey Rion, what brings you out here?" she asked as she forced a smile and fumbled to pull her sleeve over her mark.

"That's a stupid question," Rion frowned. "I came to check up on you and your garden. Both are full of pure beauty and radiance."

"We should really get going now," Verthandi's voice echoed in Morrigan's head. Morrigan was about to respond when they heard an ear-piercing screech.

"What the devil was that?" Rion started to ask but was suddenly cut short by a rain of fire that was followed closely by three dragons descending from the sky. The largest of them had golden scales and pale blue eyes. Although it had four legs, when it descended it lowered itself onto its hind two. As it touched down on land, it took on a humanoid appearance as its large girth and wings seemed to shrivel like raisins retreating into their new form.

Its large claws reduced to hands and feet and the golden scales became red armour with black streaks through it. The dragon's mane disappeared underneath the person's armour, but their eyes continued to glow light blue. He spoke something they couldn't make out to the other two dragons which were still smaller than he was in his human form.

A wide grin spread across his face as he watched the town burn. People were running around, screaming and wailing trying to put distance between themselves and the dragon. However, Sol pointed towards the town to dispatch the two dragonlings to intercept the people and ensure that none got very far. At this point he turned, and his eyes focused on Rion and Morrigan.

"Stragglers huh? Well, we can't have those." As he took several steps towards the pair Rion took one step back with his right foot and drew a sword.

"Morrigan! Get out of here, I'll hold him off!" Rion yelled without taking his sight off Sol.

"Are you *crazy*?" Morrigan shrieked at Rion whose blade did not waver from the centre of his line of sight.

"Yes, he is, but I suggest we take him up on it," Verthandi echoed.

Morrigan's body froze in place even though she was trying to move towards Rion. "No!" Verthandi's voice boomed loud and clear in her mind, "we're getting out of here *now!*"

Despite wanting to move towards Rion, Morrigan felt her body move away from him, jetting deep into the woods. Once there she ran as fast as she could, never looking back once to see the chaos behind her.

....

Back at the town, the man stood grimacing, cross armed over Rion's body. The two dragonlings were darting back and forth through the streets in the town. Heads slowly but methodically turning back and forth, eyes focused intensely as the embers began dying out leaving behind nothing but ashes of what was once the small town.

"Lord Sol," one of them spoke, landing next to the man, with his arms crossed, face still fixated in a wide, tooth grin and eyes served as mirrors, reflecting the flames as the town burned. "There is no Essence to be had in this town. Either the Terrakonan slipped out before we arrived, or they managed to avoid the flames and survived somehow."

He let out a primal roar that shook the area before turning his vision towards the two dragonlings with a broad smirk, "No matter, we have sufficiently weakened Verthandi's presence. I doubt she will be of further irritation to us." He then extended his wings and stretched his limbs as they returned to scales and claws. With a mighty roar, Lord Sol and his two dragonlings spread their wings, ascending into the deep blue sky. Together they hovered for a moment, turned east and flew off into the horizon.

Chapter 2

"Ugh…." Morrigan groaned, squinting her eyes at the bright sunlight filtering through the window in front of her. Moving her fingers, she felt a soft material underneath her as she tried to get up from her prone position. Despite her best efforts, her body would not budge. Looking around her, she noticed the earthy, brownish red clay that surrounded her. There was nothing else to see except a green chair in a corner next to an open doorway. Despite its rustic look, the room smelled mostly like the bedding she was on which smelled of the fields she had worked in and some moss. Morrigan rubbed her forehead as she struggled to recollect the events of the past twenty-four hours.

"Ah you are awake," a gentle voice materialised behind her jolting her out of her thoughts. Snapping her head around, she faced the voice to find. A woman of short stature. Her skin was sagging, but she still managed a warm smile. Her pale skin seemed a stark contrast to her jet-black hair. She rested a thin hand on Morrigan's back, "Rest my child," she spoke softly. Her voice cracked and shook as she continued. "Your body is not used to housing the essence of a dragon. Your time of motion will come soon enough, but for now, rest so that when you do begin your journey in earnest," clenching her fist, she paused briefly, "you will never have to stop."

"Who are you?" Morrigan slurred. Despite having just woken up, she felt her eyes beginning to close and head beginning to wobble and gravitate back towards the pillow.

"Where you are going, your partner can tell you all you need to know…" the woman's voice faded to black as Morrigan fell back off into a deep sleep.

"Hey, wake up!" she heard someone nudging her.

"Huh? What?" she mumbled, slowly opening her eyes. The area was now bathed in a pale green light.

"Back here again?" Morrigan groaned.

"Yes," the gentle sigh of Verthandi answered, "I suppose Minda wants us to bond further before she helps with stabilising you." She was in a solid state, not the wispy version Morrigan had seen when they first met.

"So where *are* we anyways?" Morrigan asked as she stood up looking directly at Verthandi.

"This area is called the Ardivian Space. It is a space between the realm of Terrakonans and that of Dragons," she elucidated as she swept her arm in a large arc, motioning towards the entirety of the area. "It manifests only to those who are linked by essence." A wisp of green smoke travelled from Verthandi to Morrigan. "By this link our consciousnesses are able to call to each other, and converse."

Verthandi looked off in the distance as she continued, "Ardivian Space is an empty space, but it is coloured by the souls that inhabit it. The stronger our bond is, the more luminous it will become."

"I see…" Morrigan said slowly. "But tell me," she paused before continuing, "why not fully manifest in the realm of the Terrakonans? I'm sure dragons would have no issue in the human world."

Verthandi snapped her line of sight back to Morrigan. "Have you not heard of the Terrakonans Wars?" she barked.

Morrigan looked at Verthandi before slowly shaking her head side to side. "No… I am not even familiar with the term Terrakonans. The only time dragons even get mentioned to us are stories of the great heroes."

Verthandi slumped her posture as she looked at the ground, sighing, "I suppose having not been properly groomed you would not have heard of it." She reached out behind her projecting an image behind her. There were all manner of dragons on it. Some big, some small, some on four legs, and some seemed to just slither in mid-air. The dragons appeared to be conversing outside with several stalls scattered around and some were carrying items to and from the area. "This is Tumahab, land of the dragons," Verthandi spoke motioning towards the image. "As you can see it looks very much like one of your towns. That is because at one time my kind and your kind both lived together on good terms," she paused, closing her eyes briefly, "well as good as terms get when you have large groups of sentient beings," she chuckled. "One day, a group formed called the Dragonslayers. I never really knew where they came from, but they began blaming problems on the dragons and began to actively purge our numbers." Her voice grew deep and raspy, "Of course, we fought back, but many became enraged and slaughtered all manner of sentients, not just the offending Dragonslayers." She shook her head, "of course this led to all-out war. It lasted for over a hundred years which only ended because a human leader intervened to offer a treaty. I was not alive then, but rumour has it she had embraced both the sentients and dragon cultures and was well versed in both languages. We would be given the North, while the sentients inhabited the South. It was a good deal at the time and we agreed to stay out of each other's way unless we had special permission to cross over."

"The sentients soon excelled in various fields and the dragons became intrigued as to what their neighbours were up to. This paved the way for what we call Terrakonans. Where a sentient is purposely inhabited by a dragon's spirit to observe and see the world. This did not last long as this soon evolved into a way for both sentients and dragons to gain influence on a large scale. The Terrakonans obviously had access to dragons and cults soon began to pop up, which in and of itself was fairly harmless as far as the dragons went, however, when the sentient came to the dragon hemisphere is when things got upset."

Verthandi dropped her head, looking towards Morrigan, "some sentients had mastered all manner of skills, and being so small, they were able to do all sorts of unsavoury things which could easily go undetected. This eventually triggered the Terrakonans War. A war between dragons and their avatars to decide who was the supreme duo. According to the story, the same sentient who brokered the original treaty cast a spell that would forever separate dragons and sentients into different worlds, only allowing the two to meet in this Ardivian Space."

"So, I guess the dragons suffered from the same petty things that us humans suffer from," Morrigan said with a nervous laugh. "But why maintain a link if it causes so much trouble?"

"There was a point made that if some of the dragons managed to avoid the separation, they would cause an imbalance among the sentients. Some Terrakonans also had gotten attached to their Dragon counterparts that went beyond the mere linking of essence. So, the link was kept and we've pretty much lived independently of each other since."

"But we *saw* dragons destroy my hometown!" Morrigan yelled, throwing up her arms.

"Yes, we did, and I agree it is a bit unusual. I'm not sure how they have overcome the barrier," Verthandi groaned as she was lost in thought over the situation. "But they and their Terrakonans have overcome the barrier. Perhaps they have an unparalleled level of trust. Or perhaps they are that close to each other that their thoughts and being meld into each other."

There was an odd silence between the two once Verthandi's voice trailed off. Morrigan stepped forward and extended her hand towards Verthandi and sighed. "Well, I know a little more now than I did before," forcing a smile she added, "and I guess even if I don't really like it, we're stuck with each other."

"Indeed, we are," Verthandi extended her claw. As it touched Morrigan's hand the once dark room was transformed by a bright light and the ground took on the image of long, rolling fields as far as the eye could see in every direction.

Morrigan looked around, wide eyed and then looked back at Verthandi. "Level one?"

Verthandi snorted, "Sure," smiled weakly, "level one."

A flash occurred and Morrigan found herself back in the earthen room. The mossy smell seemed stronger than ever, yet it was somehow soothing, and she let a small content sigh slip as her fingers ran down the bedding.

"Ah you're back," Morrigan heard Minda's familiar voice, yet the form Morrigan laid eyes on was of a different being. Instead of a wrinkly old lady, the woman's skin was much smoother, and tan in complexion. She still bore the same piercing black eyes and black hair. Instead of round pupils hers were vertical ellipses with large irises. Similar to a cat, but larger. When their eyes met, Morrigan scrambled up, stumbling over the side of the bed before Verthandi seized her body from moving.

"I see you've properly bonded with your dragon now," the woman said with a slight chuckle. "Judging by that response you can see through my weak illusionary spell."

"How?" Morrigan spoke, as her fist still clutched tightly in front of her chest and her eyes never wavered from those of the woman in front of her.

"She's a Terrakonan," Verthandi echoed.

"Former… Terrakonan," the woman corrected. "My partner…. died… years ago," she winced, "however, I am able to maintain some of their powers with residual essence. Come my child," she said, extending a welcoming hand towards Morrigan, "I don't bite." Grinning, she continued, "I merely watch the youngsters grow up and pass along. My time being anything near threatening has long since passed."

Morrigan looked at the hand in front of her and then back to Minda's. "It's alright," Verthandi cut through her thoughts, "Minda is an ally." Slowly, Morrigan's tightly closed arms and hands began to open and reached out to Minda's hand. Minda did not move her hand, but as Morrigan touched Minda's hand, she flinched at the warmth, before fully clasping her hand around Minda's. Minda smiled weakly as Morrigan moved her feet to the edge of the bed so that Minda could pull Morrigan up and off the bed and on her feet.

As soon as Morrigan stood up, the women's eyes met. Nodding Minda broke their silence, "Now, sadly I believe you've probably come here seeking guidance," the woman exhaled slowly, "however, as I said before my time for being anything useful to you has long since passed." Turning, Minda looked out the window before continuing, "Besides that, there are others, ears and eyes that would harm you should you stay here. The best guidance I can give you is to find your own path. On that path you will be able to learn far more than I can ever show you from the confines of this compound."

"But all this way? For nothing?" Verthandi spoke through Morrigan.

"Sad but true," the woman shook her head, looking back at Morrigan with stretched out lips. "You have been here a full week already and they draw ever closer to finishing the job they started. Much as I'd like to help, you have already been here longer than is safe." Minda paused a moment before quickly leaving the room and closed the door behind her. As one door clicked shut, another door opened that led outside the room.

"That wasn't much use…" Verthandi sighed.

"Right," Morrigan stated absently, "Let's go back home."

Chapter 3

"Truthfully speaking, Morrigan, I don't think there will be anything left of your home," Verthandi echoed. "Gold dragons are generally not ones to show mercy."

"But I'm sure he left *something*! Perhaps even a clue as to where he went to." She hung her head speaking softly, "It's the only lead we have. Home is always a good place to start."

Verthandi sighed, "Fine, I guess there is no harm in venturing back to your home even if it is a smouldering crater in the ground."

Morrigan took a step forward before pausing. "I... have no idea where... we are, since I was forced here against my will," she pouted. "I assume *you* know the way?"

"Yes, of course," Verthandi sighed heavily. "Just follow the pathway of white flowers until the river. Once we get to the river we'll eventually get to the bridge and I'm sure you can navigate from there." Morrigan muttered the directions to confirm she had them right before she once again felt her body move without her consent.

In short order, they reached the location of Morrigan's hometown, but as they drew close, they spied men in gold and black. The armour they wore bore a standard of the same colours with the crest in the centre of a white lion bearing a shield.

"Friends of yours?" Verthandi asked as she used her sight to get a look at the group from a safe distance while remaining safely hidden in the woods.

"Sort of, they are part of the national military, the Chinis Forces, but the only time I've ever seen them is during times of conscription." Then she added in a curt mumble, "And the occasional visit from the regional forces who treat our area like some sort of punishment."

"If you're that upset with them, I can lend you some power so you can release that pent up anger…"

Morrigan flinched back, frowning, "Who told you I'm angry at them?"

"Remember, I can sense your thoughts and even though I can't access your memory as to the why, I can tell in your mind that you are upset," Verthandi responded, knocking Morrigan's head playfully.

"Right," Morrigan cringed.

"Too late," Verthandi quickly added just as Morrigan was about to move forward from her hiding spot. Before she had a chance to question the dragon, she felt a sharp point stick on her back.

"Raise your hands and get up slowly," a sharp voice ordered from behind her.

"We can take him if you want, he's not much more than a sentient with a pointy stick," Verthandi echoed.

"No! Maybe we can get something from these guys. At the very least they shouldn't try anything too threatening until they can properly identify me," she scowled.

"Are you talking to yourself?" the person behind her scoffed. He then yelled out to the others as Morrigan got to her feet. "We got a live one over here!" Some of the soldiers stationed at the gate quickly made their way over towards Morrigan. One of those who came over had extended wings on his badge and wore a deeper gold than the others. He narrowed his eyes at Morrigan and slowly walked around her a few times, looking her over from top to bottom before speaking.

"You don't seem to be any threat," he muttered, "but do you know what happened here?" he asked standing in front of Morrigan, crossed arms, his mouth edges protruding downwards.

"Would you believe me if I said a dragon?" Morrigan responded without much of a pause between the question and answer.

"I certainly wouldn't believe you," Verthandi chimed.

"Normally I wouldn't, but we spotted what appeared to be a faerie on the way here," he then looked away and muttered under his breath, "or at least some form of flying humanoid."

"A faerie?" Morrigan asked. "How do you know it was a faerie?"

"If you expect me to believe your story about a dragon, then it would do you well to believe our story about seeing a faerie," the man barked at Morrigan.

"Okay, okay," Morrigan said, raising her hands.

"Faeries? I think they saw other Terrakonans, but I don't sense any nearby," Verthandi echoed in Morrigan's mind.

"Maybe the Terrakonans have figured out a way to block others from detecting them. Which means they may be hostile to us?"

"No. Golds are not one to hide. If it was him or his allies, they would broadcast themselves. It's more than likely other Terrakonans are hiding from them, but who is it that they have allowed themselves to be seen by these sentients?"

"Maybe it really is a faerie that led them to my hometown?"

"Unlikely, the fae simply do not exist. They are only seen in hallucinations or under other types of influence."

"Well, we say that about dragons too, but here I am talking to one albeit in my head."

"Miss are you talking to yourself?" the soldier smirked. "Colonel, I think we got a crazy one here, she might not be as harmless as we think," Morrigan felt the point stick her in her back.

"Hey, watch where you stick that!" Morrigan yelped as she jumped away from the point and knocked the spear away from the soldier spinning around to face him. Both of their mouths were agape as their weapons fell to the ground. For a brief moment, silence was their companion before he raised his hand, pointing directly at Morrigan.

"Seize her!" he ordered. The other soldiers attempted to tackle her to the ground.

"I thought I'd mentioned this already," Verthandi interjected, "but you maintain some residual strength from me."

"Yes, I noticed," Morrigan muttered, evading the grasp of another soldier from her side.

"However, if you want, I can infuse you with enough to throw these guys around like rag dolls."

Morrigan snickered, "So they'll come back with a bigger gun next time? I think I'll pass."

"Oh of course because your reflexes aren't amazing enough as it is. By the way, jump back."

"Why?" Morrigan never got to finish her sentence before a brilliant bolt of lightning crashed down in front of her, followed by the deafening roar of thunder.

The flash blinded her, and the sound made her stagger backwards as she covered her ears while they rang from its resonance. After a few moments, her sight began to return from being completely white. Through the haze of her sight, she saw that some soldiers were also staggering around while others were out cold on the ground.

Chapter 4

"I don't know why you insist on playing with your food Verthandi," came a voice. "Are you that afraid to lose another Terrakonan? If you want I can give you a helping hand and you can be done with having to worry so much." Another bolt landed behind Morrigan so close that she felt it singe her hair and clothing.

"Enemy?" Morrigan panted as she struggled to keep her footing and regain her senses.

"No, that voice belongs to Arnhem, but I assume he's speaking through his Terrakonan… Nome. They are a very brash coupling, but not a direct enemy to us."

Morrigan's sight had now refocused, and she saw that she had been surrounded by a cage of lightning. The soldiers all lay on the ground outside and a little to her left was a woman dressed in bright orange tabard with knee length trails and brias. Her eyes and hair had a bright yellow almost whitish glow to them, which stood out more against her almond skin. She wore a smug grin on her face as she held a ball of lightning in her right hand.

"Release us!" Verthandi spoke as she made Morrigan's eyes flashed green.

"Why should we, you were about to be captured by these sentients, you clearly do not value your own Terrakonan's life if you allow them to fall to such trivial opponents," Arnhem's voice snickered through Nome.

"That's because I don't want to make a scene!" Morrigan yelled as her eyes returned back to their normal black appearance.

"Oh, your Terrakonan can suppress you. You might be worthwhile keeping alive after all," Nome sneered as Arnhem continued speaking. The lightning ball dissipated, and the cage disappeared. Her eyes reverted to their normal light green colour and her hair colouration changed to black. The sneer melted away and was replaced with a frown.

"So, you're Verthandi's new Terrakonan huh?" Morrigan felt her hair stand on the back of her neck and a chill run up her spine as Nome's gaze felt like it pierced her to the core.

"Don't let her feel your fear, she feeds off it," Verthandi echoed as she tried to reassure Morrigan. Morrigan felt her legs stiffen and she regained her composure.

"Yes, I am."

"Awh," Nome said, her frown becoming a grin, her arms unfolded, and her posture relaxed. "You will need to toughen up fast. Don't let anyone push you around, and it's probably better to get used to causing a ruckus. No Terrakonan will ever fault you for causing a commotion, and besides, it's best to not be captured by sentients. You never know which ones are aligned with Terrakonans and will endanger you."

"Speaking of which, Verthandi says she was unable to sense you."

Nome tilted her head and frowned, "Me thinks Verthandi may be suffering Joiner's Shock. My sister Kat can erect a barrier around us to prevent the Terrakonans from detecting us."

"Maybe that's the faerie the soldiers thought they saw?" Morrigan pondered.

Nome laughed, "No, she's not a faerie. An angel maybe, but not a faerie. She's not even in the area, so I doubt the soldiers would have seen her. I only flew over after detecting the power spike from Sol, and the fall of Verthandi's." She then let out a sigh and turned back towards the ruins of the town. "Sadly, I've found no trace of Sol; well except the smouldering ruins of what used to be," flexing her hand back loosely, "I presume your hometown," she added as she motioned towards the ruins of the town.

Nome's conversation was interrupted by a build-up of energy manifesting itself as little grey particles assembling in front of them. At first, they were in a ball shape, but that morphed into the shape of a tall woman. Once in shape, a flash emanating from her chest spread across her body, revealing a long pink dress and a burgundy coat. She flicked her ebony hair over her shoulder so that it fell about midway down her back as her manifestation completed. Her eyes were a similar shade of light green as Nome's.

"My dear Nome, how many times must I tell you that the barrier only prevents so much energy from being detected? Can you please refrain from using up so much energy without proper reason?" she spoke with her back to Morrigan but standing in front of Nome.

"Yes Kat," Nome sighed, "But Arnhem thought it would be good to test out the new Terrakonan, you know, make sure they're up to scratch and not just some random push over that would just result in a collapse just like the last one." Nome's posture perked up as she put her hands into fists and pumped them in front of her.

Kat shook her head and put her hands on her hips, "The newbie is barely two days old, there are many veteran Terrakonans that would shudder under you and Arnhem's might. Let her work herself into the job before you go drawing attention to the *both* of you."

"Sorry, it won't happen again…" Nome huffed as she swung her left leg in a kicking motion while looking down at the ground.

The woman ruffled Nome's hair, laughing a little, "Just keeping you safe. If I can't protect you, then who am I qualified to protect."

Turning she faced Morrigan. Her left arm folded across her waist, while her right elbow rested on her left wrist and her arm reached up to her chin. "I apologise for my sister's rough treatment." She held her hand out to Morrigan, "My name is Katherine, but everyone calls me Kat. I assume your presence here means that we are both looking for a common enemy?"

Morrigan shrugged her shoulders, "Well I don't know, I just met you after your sister tried to kill me."

Katherine laughed, "Nome and Arnhem have that effect on people. They are of the fry first, ask questions later mentality."

"Why don't we just leave her out here if she doesn't trust us," Nome scowled as she turned back around to face Morrigan. "You can't save everyone Kat, and Verthandi doesn't exactly have a glittering record either."

"What do you mean?" Morrigan snapped.

"Nome, there is no need to upset her," Katherine said in a tone causing Morrigan to feel a shiver up her spine and Nome to shrink away.

"I'm just saying, we have better things to do than babysit both dragon and Terrakonans," Nome muttered as she swung her left leg and hung her head down, arms behind her back.

A small smile formed on her lips, and when next she spoke Morrigan no longer felt the tingling up her spine, "That is no reason to discourage. You never know where allies or even enemies may come from. Sometimes no matter what you do, you can neither save yourself, nor others, but at the very least, you need to be able to give everyone a chance." Sighing, she looked off into the distance before speaking quietly to herself, "Everyone... deserves a second chance." After a few moments of looking off into the distance, her gaze returned back to Morrigan. "Are you able to fly yet?"

"Fly?" Morrigan asked as her brow creased into a long furrow and her eyes squinted at Katherine.

"I take that as a no," Katherine chuckled. "Guess its ankle express then, which probably works out for the better, more time for Dragon and Terrakonan to bond."

"We can't stay around here?" Morrigan asked.

Katherine shook her head, "No. Aside from being out in the open, we don't know if Sol will come back."

"He razed the town to the ground! What *more* can he want?" Morrigan shrieked.

"Are we *sure* we can't just dump her out here and leave her?" Nome remarked and rolled her eyes.

Katherine smiled and closed her eyes. She slowly brought her hands up to her chest. Morrigan felt the air go still and cold. A light haze formed around Katherine which solidified into two large grey wings. Morrigan noticed how the wings looked similar to Verthandi's as she pulled them back behind her. As they reached their resting place, they gently brushed against Morrigan's shoulder. They felt almost soft and silky. When Katherine opened her eyes, they took on a grey glow.

The voice that spoke from Katherine was cantankerous and Morrigan felt each word reverberate within her. "Young Terrakonan, although yours is a curious situation, you must not take it lightly. While my charge is indeed a patient one, I do not always share her sentiment. My advice is to follow her unless I will end Verthandi's presence myself and snap you in two." There was a short pause to which Morrigan stiffly nodded and a low growl escaped from Katherine before she continued. "Also, Verthandi, control your charge. Trained she might not be, but you can still at least encourage her to make proper choices that will not be detrimental to all."

"Yes, Nogomain" Verthandi's voice sighed through Morrigan.

"Good, I hope to not require this conversation… again." The voice faded as the wings receded away from Morrigan and into Katherine's back. The glow in her eyes faded and returned to their original hazel hue.

"Is that what happens when I blank out and don't remember anything?" Morrigan asked Verthandi.

"Yes, although it is unlikely, they blank out between switches. Those two, particularly Katherine and Nogomain have been together for centuries."

"But Katherine doesn't look much older than me!"

"Looks can be deceiving, remember the Terrakonans share some of the abilities of their linked dragon. One of them is longevity."

"So, I can live for *centuries* like this?"

"Perhaps, if we can get past this initial stage."

"You don't sound very confident," Morrigan said, puffing her cheeks and pouting.

"I hate to interrupt your conversation, but as we mentioned earlier, we'd like to move away from this area," Katherine said with a little cough.

"How?"

"Your posture froze, and your eyes glazed over," Katherine chuckled. "Means you're newly linked. When you get along better with your dragon your body doesn't freeze from the sudden surge when the dragon invades your mind."

"Or you develop habits that better hide it," Nome snapped. She was going to say more but was cut off by Katherine's raised hand. Katherine looked towards the East for a few moments before refocusing back on the group.

"Away, *now!*" Before anyone could respond she grabbed both Nome and Morrigan's arms and began walking forward.

Chapter 5

Her wings quickly began to form and just as Morrigan felt as if she was going to trip, they lifted off the ground. It was not a high flight; Katherine flew just above the tree line. Morrigan thought it was perhaps due to the weight of carrying her and Nome, however, as they cleared the tree line, Katherine released Nome as she spread her own wings and flew alongside. Unlike Katherine's wings, Nome's wings were two pairs of smaller wings made up of a feather-like material that glowed a faint reddish orange.

"I think we found our fairy," Morrigan spoke to Verthandi.

"You think Nome looks like a fae?" There was a short pause before Verthandi continued, "Perhaps, it fits in with the sentient description."

The rest of the trip was fairly quiet. Katherine did not acknowledge any of Morrigan's questions and seemed fixed on what was straight ahead. Nome flew in her tailwind and said nothing for the duration of the trip.

The shadows were long as Katherine descended back to the ground onto a clearing. To Morrigan it looked as if her wings extended a bit further as she glided down and landed with a gentle thud. Morrigan fell to the ground as they landed since she was unable to keep her footing.

"Guess I should have mentioned the few steps needed on landing," Katherine said as she stretched her wings out across the entire width of the clearing before allowing them to recede into her back. She then added with a chuckle, "Nogomain says you're going to have fun when Verthandi teaches you to fly." The comment was met with a groan as Morrigan got to her feet and dusted herself off. "By the way, I'd move from there if I were you."

"Why?" Morrigan asked as Katherine pointed upwards. Morrigan followed her finger up and saw Nome was circling above the treeline. She watched as Nome climbed a little higher with a few wing flaps before wrapping her arms and wings tightly around herself and began plummeting towards the ground at increasing speed. Morrigan dove out of the way just as Nome quickly extended her wings and extremities to come to a stop just above the ground in a cloud of dust.

"Was that really necessary?" Morrigan coughed.

"Of course, it was," Nome smiled. "Gotta keep the reflexes sharp." She stretched her wings and arms out before they melted away.

"Should have gotten you to bring down some moss or something before you came down," Katherine remarked as she turned around to the other two.

"Why?" Nome shrugged. "We always sleep fine under the stars without much cover."

Katherine sighed and rubbed her head, "We do, yes, but can Morrigan?"

"Of course, she can, why wouldn't she?"

Katherine ignored Nome and instead addressed Morrigan, "Verthandi, you know better than us all, is Morrigan steeled enough to survive outside overnight? There are clouds, so it shouldn't be a freezing night, but it will still be pretty cold, given sentient biology and all."

Morrigan's eyes went green as Verthandi spoke, "I don't know. She is untested in the elements. I don't feel my powers are particularly strong with her yet. Perhaps some minimal warmth should suffice."

"I'd rather not make a fire, would make it easy to spot even in the middle of the woods," Katherine responded.

"If she can sleep with some tingling, I can arrange for a mild electrical blanket from Arnhem. But we really should have thought this through before starting," Nome chimed in.

"Well Katherine gave us little room for pause," Verthandi rebuffed.

"Yeah Kat, just what was with that quick ascent?" Nome frowned and crossed her arms.

Katherine blinked a few times, "Did neither of you detect them?"

"Who?" Verthandi and Nome echoed.

"Stop fooling around Nome," Katherine laughed nervously.

Nome scowled at Katherine, and she stopped laughing. Her jaw dropped. "You... really didn't notice?"

"For the third time, no!" Nome yelled.

"The Rannsoknardomari..." Katherine spoke slowly, almost unable to keep her mouth from gaping.

"Oh, them. Didn't Charlie kill them all some centuries back?" Morrigan responded as her eyes changed to green.

"No, never. Where did you hear that story from?" Katherine asked as she furrowed her brow.

"Were you not at the council when they discussed our old enemies had been disbanded? Not that they really could do anything without the physical presence of dragons on this plane. Or maybe your caretaker has left you in the dark."

"Do *not* speak out of turn," Nogomain hissed as Katherine's eyes flashed grey. "I am aware of what happened in the council as is my charge. Unlike you who cannot seem to keep your charges, I share information with mine and she is well aware of things in light and in shadow."

"My being able to keep charges has nothing to do with their ignorance! I ward mine as you ward yours, perhaps if you took a more progressive stance on things, you wouldn't feel so safe either," Verthandi hissed back.

"Stop! Both of you!" Nome yelled as she stood between them and held them apart. They both leered at each other for a few more moments before Katherine backed off.

"We will finish this discussion in Tumahab."

"Agreed," Verthandi growled. Both backed away from Nome and their eye colouration returned to normal. Katherine closed her eyes and exhaled slowly while Morrigan gasped and took a few steps back.

"You two simmered down?" Nome demanded as Katherine opened her eyes and Morrigan took a few moments to catch her breath.

"I do wish he wouldn't be so blunt with himself," Katherine sighed. She then looked over to Morrigan, "We'll make camp; hopefully those two can sort themselves out in Tumahab so that we don't regress to petty arguing." She then moved out of the clearing without saying another word.

"Where is she going?" Morrigan asked Nome.

"Probably to get some moss to make bedding and some covers. Which reminds me, I need to test your reaction to electricity," she said, raising her hands up to shoulder height. "Let me know if you feel anything, or if it becomes unbearable." Morrigan nodded and Nome started her test charging.

At first Morrigan didn't feel or see anything. After a moment she felt a tingling sensation as her hair began to stick up and attract towards Nome. A few minutes later she saw a faint orange-yellow glow emanating from Nome's hand, forming a line up and around her head, down her back to her ankles and back to Nome. The orange glow then gave way to a light purple hue and her hair seemed to relax a little more. It felt a little warm, almost soothing. As the hue started to take on a bluish hue, she felt a stinging sensation and the smell of smoke wafted up to her nostrils.

"Stop!" she yelled. Nome immediately broke off the charge and Morrigan brushed through her hair making sure there were no burnt or split ends.

"Not bad," Nome laughed to herself.

"What's with that smug grin?" Morrigan demanded.

"Nothing," Nome responded, still grinning. "There may be hope for you yet." Nome said, snapping her fingers, "Oh you'll probably want to eat something soon." She put her hands in her pocket and brought out two items.

"Fireballs?" Morrigan remarked noting the red shape and green tailings.

"No!" Nome laughed. "Granted if I could keep fire in my pocket that would be *amazing*! They are weirdly enough called dragon fruits, and they are very tasty when toasted." She gave one to Morrigan and kept the other.

"Place your hands like this," she said as she covered the top with one hand and the bottom with the other, laying the green tailings between her wrists. Morrigan did as she was told and then looked back at Nome once her hands were in position.

"Ok, now with *all* your might, turn your hands in opposite directions, like you're opening a jar." Again, Morrigan did as she was told, but try as she might, nothing happened other than it felt like she was rubbing her hand against hard rubber. After a few tries, she looked up to see Nome watching her with a big grin on her face.

"That's not how you do it is it?" Morrigan frowned, to which Nome doubled over with laughter.

"Nome what are you doing?" Katherine sighed as she returned to the clearing with some green moss mats. Nome by now had dropped on the ground laughing and Morrigan turned to face Katherine, showing her the dragon fruit.

"Oh, that," Katherine rolled her eyes.

"I'm sorry Kat, I couldn't resist," Nome said, wiping a tear from her eye. Katherine dropped the mats near Morrigan and took the fruit from her.

"Believe it or not, for all the fanciness, the fruit opens up more like a banana," Katherine said as she grabbed one of the green tailings and pulled down on the tip of it. The skin easily peeled away, exposing the black spotted white fruit beneath. She then handed it back to Morrigan, "You can eat it raw, or you can let Nome zap it a little. It's a little sweet, but it's not a bad taste for something that gives quite an energy boost when you don't have a real meal."

"Thanks," Morrigan said as she started peeling off the red of the skin.

"By the way V, the skin is edible," Nome said as she had finally recovered enough to lie still on the ground face up. She held up her hand and pointed at Morrigan's fruit. Before Morrigan could say anything, a bolt of lightning jumped from Nome's pointer finger to Morrigan's fruit. She flinched and dropped it as she heard it sizzle and pop, but Nome caught it before it hit the ground. "Now don't go wasting my food *and* my time," Nome said as she got to her feet and returned the fruit to Morrigan.

"Sorry… I was just… surprised…" Morrigan said softly as she accepted the fruit back from Nome without making eye contact. She looked at it for a few moments as it was still smoking a little.

"If you're not going to eat it, I'll eat both of them," Nome said as she began eating hers.

"Oh, no, I'll eat it," Morrigan said, and took a bite. Her first bite gave her pause as the mixture of sweet flavour and gritty texture swamped her mouth. Such was her pause that some of the juice ran down her chin which she quickly wiped up with her sleeve. "Thank you, Nome," she said finally after taking a few bites.

"No problem," Nome said, finishing her own fruit. She began to arrange the moss mats on the ground as makeshift bedding. As she did, Morrigan noticed the familiar smell. The bedding in Minda's house.

Once Morrigan finished her fruit, she lowered herself to the ground, allowing her knees to rest gently on the grass as she helped Nome spread out the mats. She took a deep breath in, letting the smell flood her nostrils, her mind and body felt as if being wrapped in the softest of cloth. Before she knew it, she had her head on the ground as another contented sigh slipped from her lips, her eyes closed, and she drifted off to sleep.

It was pitch black, and the air was still when Morrigan woke up. She had no idea what time it was as she reached up and felt dampness on the mossy cover. As she sat up, she felt the cold air whip around her upper body, and quickly pulled the covering up to her face. Looking around she saw Nome sprawled out, face up, partially under her covering. She was laughing to herself although clearly asleep. Morrigan smiled absently. Typical Nome, always laughing to herself, no doubt still on about the dragon fruit.

Then she became aware of a faint sound in the distance. She craned her neck and held her breath to try hearing if the sound was... something... or just the wind. For a few moments she listened before faintly, she heard it again. Singing? It certainly was a voice, but to whom did it belong? She got up to follow the tune but was careful not to disturb Nome.

Slowly, she inched towards the edge of the clearing, stepping on her tippy toes, putting her feet down almost in the same spot to avoid rustling the vegetation any more than she had to. At the edge of the clearing, the sound became a little clearer. It was Katherine's voice. Soft, melodic and gentle as the wind that lightly brushed her cheek just as it was earlier that day when Katherine first had addressed her. Morrigan listened for a moment longer to better pinpoint the direction of the voice and moved into the woods to follow the sound. As she got closer, Katherine's voice became more defined, and fuller but remained a mezzo-soprano. Her steps quickened as she felt Katherine's voice becoming clearer until the woods opened back up into another clearing.

This clearing opened up into a large lake. The water was perfectly still, the moon and the stars in the sky almost a mirror reflection of each other. On the nearby bank, she found Katherine sitting on a rock, her back was towards Morrigan, slowly swaying to the tune she was singing, eyes dancing across the sky.

Dragons, what a time to be alive. With the Council of Ta'lel, a golden age will thrive.

Dragons, do remind. That time does not rewind.

Though ageless to the world. Time continues to unfurl.

Mistakes can be wrought. Through times without thought.

With Terrakonans we plea. A faithful decree.

Where in our strength we can rely. And align.

That history will not repeat. Where we hang our heads in defeat.

Dragon and Terrakonans. Tied by Ardivian.

Before wondering blind. Now two souls bind.

Towards the light we march. Ever forward til we find ourselves under the timeless arch.

Katherine lowered her gaze across the lake and then spoke plainly, "Couldn't sleep or did Nome's ruckus wake you up?"

Morrigan approached Katherine and stood next to her, "No, I slept well," gazing up at the stars she took a deep breath and clasped her hands in front of her. "At least I think I did. Nome didn't bother me, but she was smirking, so who knows what was going on with her."

Katherine laughed while stirring the water with her feet. "Nome is a mischievous person, but the one thing she does not mess with is sleep. Don't judge her too badly though. As troublesome as she can sometimes be, she's the best ally you ever want to have in a pinch. Also, you have to remember that some of that is probably shaped and encouraged by Arnhem." Tapping the area next to her, she looked at Morrigan and spoke, "If you're going to stay up, might as well take a seat. Nome won't be up for a while yet and it's unusual to have someone to talk to until Nogomain comes back."

"Comes back?" Morrigan tilted her head as she sat down.

"Yes, our night is the active time for the dragons. Just like us, to a degree, when they communicate through us, their bodies become immobile. So, during their active time they go around and do what dragons do, and then when they are inactive, they check in on us."

"How do you know all this?"

"Nogomain showed me some things and we talk a lot. I think it a little one sided that they can disrupt us, but we're not able to disrupt them." Chuckling she added, "I guess disrupting them mid-flight would be a problem though."

Morrigan let out a long sigh and fell back to a supine position, arms extending back over her head. "So much to learn, it's exhausting."

"It is," Katherine said as she raised her legs out of the water. "Even now after all these years I can't say I know everything, but it took a long time to know what I do know and who knows how much is actually true since I can't physically or spiritually manifest myself in Tumahab to see things for myself."

"Uh-huh…." Morrigan said forlornly before sitting up again and continuing, "That song you were singing when I got out here. What was it?"

"It's a Travelin Song. According to Nogomain they are short tunes meant to break up the long monotony of long journeys. He is very fond of them and will sing them if we're out investigating or he knows I'm doing something I don't want to be disturbed with."

"He doesn't seem like a singing dragon, at least not the same type of singer as you."

Katherine laughed, "He's a terrible singer. But that doesn't stop him. It's always slightly off key and I think he tries to sing in my register instead of his own."

"He doesn't seem like that type of dragon. He seems rather cantankerous and always serious."

"And that is where you are wrong," Katherine chortled. She leaned forward a little, looking up at the starry night sky. She closed her eyes and grinned, "Dragons are no different than people; we all have different traits and characteristics. Some things we only show after you get to know another for an extended period of time, while some things you are happy to show perfect strangers. He likes to come over as serious and cantankerous; it makes him feel safe." She then took in a deep break and leaned back a little as she stirred the water with her legs, "Nome's initial response is to play tricks or convince with sufficient amounts of electricity." She then brought her gaze back to Morrigan and placed her hands in her lap, a smile crept across her face with a hint of laughter, "Think about it, Nome tricked you with the dragon fruit, but you can't say your sleep was disrupted, nor did she burn you once she knew your heat limit."

The first rays of sunlight began creeping across the sky as Morrigan nodded her head. Katherine pulled her feet out of the water and after shaking them off, dried them with the seam of her dress.

"Nogomain is going to be late," she said with a sigh before adding, "Let's get back to camp. While I don't think Nome will wake up of her own volition anytime soon, we might need to get an early start to get to Garlot."

Chapter 6

"The capital?" Morrigan asked, getting to her feet and dusting her butt off. "But wouldn't we be easier targets there?"

"Not really," Katherine responded as she stepped off. "A bigger city means bigger crowds to hide in. We'll also probably need to search the library for a few things."

"I see..."

"Don't worry so much; just treat this as a trip to better yourself." They arrived at camp where Nome still slept, sprawled out with a wide smile on her face, just as Morrigan left her. Katherine nudged Nome's left side with her foot. "Rise and shine sleepy head!"

Nome tried to roll over to her right side, but Katherine kept her foot planted on Nome's side to prevent her from rolling, "Five more minutes..." she groaned as she raised her hand to shield her eyes from the slowly rising sun.

"Nope, we need to get back to Garlot ASAP to finish off our research." Nome groaned again and moved Katherine's foot off her side, slowly getting to her feet.

"Why so early though…" Nome said, stretching and letting out the biggest yawn. She scratched the crown of her head. Her hair was dishevelled. Morrigan tried to reach out and brush it in place, but all she got for her hard work was a zap of electricity.

"Ow!" she flinched back and rubbed her hand that got zapped.

"Don't touch the hair, it'll fix itself once I wake up," Nome yawned again.

"Has Arnhem checked in with you yet?" Katherine interrupted.

"This morning? No. He said there was supposed to be a big meeting at the council that he was going to attend." Nome changed her pose and frowned, "I'm guessing Nogomain hasn't come back either?"

"No," Katherine shook her head. "How about you Morrigan, have you heard from Verthandi?" Morrigan shook her head.

"Alright, let's make haste to Garlot. That research we were doing might be even more valuable than we think if they don't come back," Katherine said. She was about to turn around to walk off when an arrow whizzed past her.

"You two are going nowhere!" a voice yelled as ten people surrounded them. Four had crossbows trained on them, four others had fireballs at the ready and the last two had short swords drawn in one hand with a shield in the other. They were all clad in dark grey armour with red highlights along the edges and seams. A crest of a dragon with two crossed swords going through it was on the shields of the two with swords.

"Sleepless night?" Katherine asked as she raised her hands. Morrigan followed suit but Nome kept her hands down.

"I didn't do anything! Please don't hurt me!" Morrigan wailed.

"We're not here for you, we're here for your kidnappers," one of the archers yelled. "Now Terrakonans release your prisoner to us, and we can end this without further pain or suffering."

"But –"Morrigan was about to protest when Katherine stepped on her toe.

"Quiet, they don't know you're one of us. Go with them, you'll be safer at least for the immediate time. Me and Nome will be fine, it's not our first run in with them," Katherine whispered without taking her eyes off the advancing swordsman.

"Who are they?"

"They are the Rannsoknardomari... the Dragon Killers."

"But won't they kill me?" Morrigan gasped.

"No, not right away at least. They do not know you are the same as us. Use it to your advantage. Chances are they will take you back to Garlot. If they do, meet us at the Grand Archival Library."

"We could just take them on," Nome whispered. "It's not an army."

"No. They would dominate us without our full abilities. And no offence to Morrigan, but she'd be an easy target that they would so happily use as leverage if she were to get seriously injured or die. Just go along with the plan. Let's get Morrigan to safety first, and then we can handle the rest."

Nome sighed and slowly raised her hands, "I don't know why you go so far out of your way to help, when a more direct approach would be better for all."

Morrigan did as she was told and surrendered. One of the mages escorted Morrigan out of the clearing, while a swordsman and mage each bound Nome and Katherine's wrists as one of the archers approached. His armour was heavier than the others present, and he wore a torn red cape with a black outline that made it look worn and ragged. He had a large scar across his face and wore an eye patch. Katherine's mouth gaped and eyes widened as he approached.

"Nome and Katherine Mamoragan, you two are indeed a tough duo to track; I could not believe my luck to know you had made an overnight camp. Doubtless to say I probably have your prisoner to thank for that."

"Gilbert, why are you with the Slayers? I thought you were..."

"Dead?" he smirked. He then pointed to his scar, "Not quite. I need only to look at my face every day to remember how close it came but the reaper would not have me. Not until I killed those who took my best friend and turned her against me."

Katherine's face took on an angered state and Morrigan saw her body language jerk as her restrained hands failed to break free. "What happened between us is strictly between us. Why involve the order and Nome in your quest for vengeance?"

He took an arrow out of his quiver and ran it under his nose before pointing it at Katherine. "A Dragonslayer, poison more potent than ever. I was disappointed you surrendered without a fight; it seems as if your partner is not with you. It is he whom I have a quarrel with. You will yet live until I can drive this through your heart, so he can watch as I do."

"Oh, come *on* Gilbert, this lovers' spat was *aeons* ago. Go find yourself another woman," Nome scoffed. Gilbert looked at Nome for a quick second before knocking her to the ground with a swift back hand.

"You be quiet! You have no right to talk to me like that!" he yelled. "It is only by my mercy that you yet live."

"Katherine is my sister! Her business is my business," Nome spat. "Whether you like it or not, she did not choose you. Be a man and grow up!"

Gilbert let out a scream before falling down on Nome and driving the arrow through her chest. His face contorted to a smirk, "Always the loud one, now understand why your sister always tried to control you."

"Better than believing in a lie," Nome gasped before spitting in his face. Gilbert was about to twist the shaft when Katherine pushed him off Nome.

"Nome…" she said quietly, tears started to form in her eyes and run down her face.

"It's ok Kat," she wheezed. "Sisters stick up for each other. If we can't do that, what good are we to each other."

Katherine was kneeling next to Nome, their foreheads touching when a grey misty haze began to form. It was barely noticeable, like light smoke. "I'm so sorry Nome, you were right, I was wrong." She whispered more under her breath, but none heard.

"He's here," Gilbert smiled as he got to his feet. He loaded an arrow into his crossbow and pointed it at Katherine.

Nogomain's laugh could be heard as Katherine remained kneeling over Nome. "Foolish mortal, you have made a deadlier enemy than me this day. Sisters they may be, but mother and child they are. And you like so many in your order before you have made the mistake of attacking the child."

"Shut up and die!" Gilbert yelled as he shot the arrow. The arrow did not reach Katherine and stopped as if stuck in the haze.

"Fire *everything*!" He ordered those with him, and the remaining troops fired everything available to them at Katherine, kicking up a lot of dust intermingled with the haze. He raised his hand after a few moments to allow the dust to clear. As the dust cleared, he saw one large wing covering Katherine and Nome. It peeled back to reveal Katherine, her eyes glowing golden, and free of her bindings. Her skin had taken on a metallic look, and she had grown a tail.

"Know that your enemy is from within. This day you have crossed the line beyond no return, and you shall wish you truly had died all those years ago," she said as she stood up carrying Nome's limp body in her arms. "Today you will learn that there are fates worse than death, and there are greater things than your crusade against an unknown enemy."

"Restrain her!" Gilbert ordered again as she spread her wings. Katherine collapsed them around her to guard herself from a sphere that they were forming around her, trying to compress her into a space. At first it looked like the ball was starting to shrink her until in one blast she repelled and released all the energy in a huge wave of power knocking everyone and everything around her to the ground. In one giant flap she flew high into the sky and again, extended her wings, allowing them to catch the sunlight as if they were solar panels.

"Soulless one, your nightmare has just begun. Surrender your mind, that it be forever blind. Black as night, forever in flight. Never shall you find rest under the eternal arches, until first you find a soul whom can guide your marches." She then released the energy stored in her wings and all on the ground were engulfed in a golden light, before everything went black.

Chapter 7

Morrigan felt someone nudging her. "Hey, wake up," the voice sounded distant. She groaned a few times and tried to open her eyes before she heard the voice again, closer and clearer.

"Verthandi…" she said slowly, opening her eyes. The dragon was looking down, over her. The ground beneath her felt hard and the sky was grey and cloudy.

"Good you're awake, however I must quickly withdraw."

"Huh? Why?" Morrigan said, dazed. "I just got up."

"You are with the Rannsoknardomari. If they find your link you could possibly be killed. They seem to be preoccupied with Nome and Katherine's fate for now. I will keep at a distance at least until you get into the city and away from them. If they ask to examine you, decline. With my abilities I can heal you back to normal."

"Ok…" She said, trying to sit up but fell down as her head spun.

"Don't push yourself, rest and don't let them pry too much. I will be near, but I can't assimilate."

"Ok," Morrigan responded. Verthandi began to fade away, but as she did, Morrigan noticed a smile flashed across Verthandi's face and a small break in the clouds. "I hope they're alright…" she whispered as she closed her eyes. The ground beneath her softened and she became aware of an intensifying pain in her arms. Burning, searing pain, and a weight on her chest. She screamed as she sat up, grabbing her arms and looking around. She was in a stone room with a single large window allowing natural light in the room. There was not much in the way of furnishings in the room, and it seemed a little warm.

"You're awake, finally!" a man breathed a sigh of relief and fixed his glasses as he sat back away from Morrigan's bed.

"Where am I?" Morrigan asked as her sight fell on the man.

"You're at Akranes Outpost in Garlot. You were rescued when we went out to investigate dragon activity." He paused and gazed out the window. "Sadly, only you and Commander Gilbert survived. Everyone was dead when we got there." He then looked back at Morrigan, "However, you don't seem to be of the same mind of Gilbert. Perhaps you can tell the council what happened."

Morrigan furrowed her brow, "What do you mean… same mind?"

"Commander Gilbert suffers some form of dark vision anytime he closes his eyes. He doesn't even have to be asleep. His mind clouds with dragons burning down and destroying his village, the country, and even the world."

"But dragons don't exist in our plane. Aren't we taught that they were all banished after the wars?"

The man chuckled to himself, "That's what everyone would have you believe. But if that was the case, our order wouldn't need to exist."

"Which order is that? I admit no one introduced me before being blasted…" Morrigan wanted to say more but found her speech actively impeded and she was unable to continue the sentence past that point.

"Oh, how terrible of me!" the man exclaimed, "Our order is the Rannsoknardomari. The Dragon Slayers." He then pointed to himself, "My name is Charlie Derby. Our job is to completely eradicate dragon activity in our world, be it from a dragon or Terrakonans."

"My name is Morrigan Bloom. But do either really cause that much trouble?" Morrigan asked.

Charlie nodded his head, "Indeed they do. Every so often they either use their power to outright bring chaos to civilization or they use their power to empower themselves as false gods in this world." He then clenched his fist and looked upwards, "The dragons seem to be more active as of late though. We received word of a destroyed village a fortnight ago and the attack that you got caught up in two days ago. This is the time I've been waiting for to be able to fight against a real dragon and perhaps make a name for myself!"

"But isn't it dangerous? What happens if you don't make it?"

Charlie's posture dropped as he lowered his hands and looked at the ground. "My family is all dead," he said quietly. "Killed for speaking out against a Terrakonan."

"I'm… sorry to hear that…" Morrigan said softly.

"It's ok," he said as he raised his head. "I use that as motivation to keep going, knowing that one day I will be able to have vengeance on those who took so much. I may be a simple healer now, but one day I will be among the elites who finally put an end to these Terrakonans."

"I'm sure you can," Morrigan said with a nervous laugh.

Charlie then got up and stretched. "But I better go for now. I will inform the council you are awake and responsive. As the sole sentient survivor, I'm sure they'll want to know what exactly happened." He closed the door behind him, leaving the room eerily quiet with the exception of a few birds singing outside.

"Ugh, they are putting you before the council," Verthandi interrupted the quietness.

"Another interrogation, at least they don't suspect anything yet," Morrigan sighed as she curled up on the bed.

"Not yet, and don't give them any reason to. If they ask anything too serious, just put it down to luck. Luck and fate. Sentients seem to like throwing those reasons into everything."

"Not all," Morrigan snapped back. "I can't say luck or fate lead me to Katherine and Nome."

"You could, except you don't have a reason for such things. They will ask that question, and just say they caught you escaping from a destroyed village."

"I can't say that! That would frame them as destroyers of the village, and I *know* it wasn't them!"

"Then what other reason do you have? It is the easiest route to take without implicating yourself."

Morrigan curled herself tighter, "I know... but after seeing how they just killed Nome in cold blood, I don't think it would be right to then falsely accuse Katherine of the village's destruction."

"Then accuse Nome. She's dead and they can't do anything more to her."

"But did you see Charlie's zeal? I'd be making my own life harder." Her eyes began to water as she continued, "Even if Nome is dead and unable to defend herself, implicating a Terrakonan for something they didn't do will only serve to fuel them more."

"Either way a dragon did it," Verthandi sighed. "You'd just be postponing the inevitable. Not to mention you'd still have to come up with an excuse."

"No! Maybe... that's it!" Morrigan said as she uncurled and looked blankly at the ceiling. "Fate. Fate would bring me here to help them."

"Are you *crazy*?" Verthandi yelled.

"No. They say the best place to hide is right under their nose. They'd never think one so bold as to infiltrate their own ranks."

"And what if you're caught? You'd be killed on the spot!"

"We'll cross that bridge when we get there..." Morrigan said dryly. "For now, it's the only place to learn about what looks like the biggest obstacle to living. Eventually they'll figure something out but learning their ways will give us an edge when the time comes to run." Morrigan then heard footsteps approaching the door.

"I still think this is a crazy idea, but I'll have to trust you for now. Don't get yourself killed," Verthandi said as Morrigan felt her presence fade away. Morrigan took in a deep breath and released it as she heard the door open.

"I present to you the Council of Telleh," Charlie said as he entered the room and braced himself stiffly. He was followed by four people. They all wore the same red and black armour that she had seen the others wear during the fight with Katherine and Nome. The first was a large man who nearly took up the entire door frame as he passed through. He was the only one still wearing his helmet, thus he was completely covered in armour and Morrigan was unable to see any defining features of him.

The second was another man of average height and build. His skin was very pale, and his face was drawn. His posture wasn't as rigid as the others, and he walked with a slight hunch. His hair was black with streaks of white and grey.

The third person was a woman with striking fiery red hair and green eyes. She was slightly taller than the second man. Unlike the others, her armour was completely red without the black highlights. Her face showed no emotion, or at the very least did not betray her thoughts one way or another to Morrigan.

The last person who entered was a small man, he was at least a head shorter than the second man, but he was stout. He entered with a scowl on his face as he took up his position next to the woman, his black eyes staring intently on Morrigan.

Chapter 8

Once all four were in the room, the woman stepped forward and addressed Morrigan, "As announced, we are the Council of Telleh, and we guide the Rannsoknardomari to victory. My name is Solara Siren, my comrade on the end is Supreme Commander Milotis Ragnor, next to him is Deputy Commander Ryan Coddington and on my left is Vaan Doko. We do not normally hold meetings outside our chambers, but the situation has escalated quickly, and we need to form a rapid response to it."

"What exactly is going wrong?" Morrigan asked.

"Ryan? Do you want to explain?" the woman said, looking to her right, taking a step back.

"Certainly," Ryan said, stepping forward and clearing his throat. "We have reason to believe after aeons, the dragons are starting to move on a project that will once again unite Tumahab with our world," he spoke plainly with an almost stony gaze looking towards Morrigan. His hand behind his back, and his posture perfectly erect as he continued, "Currently the two are separated by something the Terrakonans refer to as Ardivian Space. According to research this space was created because simple division did not succeed in fully separating man from dragon. The dragons constructed with the help of their Terrakonans a portal that could link both worlds called Asterian Gate. The gates could pass through one medium, but two mediums were said to stop it, hence the buffer afforded us by Ardivian

Space." He paused and looked towards the window briefly and grit his teeth before setting his gaze back on Morrigan, "However, the gate's location itself is lost to us, and we have received reports that the dragons are trying to enhance this gate's abilities by offering souls from slaughtered towns and cities."

"What you're saying is," Morrigan paused a moment as she pursed her lips and folded her hands in her lap, "that we could face a Dragon War?"

"Precisely," Solara responded as she again stepped forward, and Ryan fell back in line. "You were with the Terrakonans Nome and Katherine when Gilbert's Team fell to them." She narrowed her eyes at Morrigan, her mouth contorting to a scowl as her pitch dipped, "We checked your background and have found that you inhabited one of the villages they destroyed. Yet that does not fully explain why you were with them, and they didn't kill you with the rest of your townsfolk." She brought her arms to rest on the bed's footboard and spoke almost in a hiss, "Who are you and why were you spared when everyone else died?"

Morrigan thought for a moment. Although she assured Verthandi she would use a fate defence, the term had not come up at all in the conversation thus far. Her mind scrambled to come up with something to tell Solara and soon she had a recollection.

"They said they needed me for research at the Grand Library and Archives." Solara's mouth dropped for a moment at the revelation and the three behind her all looked at each other.

Solara stood back up and looked over towards Milotis and he nodded. Her scowl melted back to a grin as she refocused back on Morrigan. "Since we suspect that one or both Terrakonans are still alive since Gilbert is wrecked with some spell which they no doubt cast on him, and it's likely you certainly want to get some payback to those who destroyed your town taking you out of your normal life, would you scout the library for us? We do not know what Nome and Katherine look like, but you know them, and they know you. They let it slip, they are going to the library, so it should be a good plan to bait them out with you. What say you?"

"It sounds harmless enough…" Morrigan thought. "I'm not in any immediate danger though, am I?"

"Well," Solara took a deep breath, "dealing with Terrakonans is always a dangerous job, but if you want, we can assign a protector to keep you safe should they lash out."

"Okay, I agree," Morrigan nodded.

"Splendid!" Solara clapped. "By the looks of it, tomorrow you should be ready to go." Morrigan nodded. "Excellent." Solara turned, facing Charlie, "Make sure she's up and mobile by tomorrow. The sooner we can get this underway, the sooner we can learn more about the Terrakonans movements."

"Aye ma'am," Charlie saluted.

"For now, we take our leave. Thank you for your cooperation," Solara said with a polite bow before turning around and going through the door. The other three followed her out and closed the door behind them.

Once they had left, Charlie let out his breath and released his salute. "You're not very good with the saluting thing, are you?" Morrigan asked.

"Deportment and etiquette are important for getting ahead," Charlie responded. "But you've been here for two days and already got an assignment from the council, you should feel honoured."

"Honoured or scared?" Morrigan said with a shiver.

"Definitely honoured," Charlie responded. "Terrakonans are a scary bunch, and some will pay the ultimate price, but like our song says: 'the bold will fight on. Until there is nothing left of their existence but an echo of song.'

Morrigan cringed, "You mean to kill them all? They can't *all* be bad, can they?"

"Yes, they are *all* bad. I have never come across a merciful or a helpful Terrakonan. The only time you hear about them is when they show up to destroy or kill things." He then sighed heavily, "Your town was destroyed by a Terrakonan, you watched a slaughter happen at the hands of a Terrakonans. How can any good come from something so savage?"

"Well, I can't admit to knowing *all* the living Terrakonans, so…"

Charlie raised his hand, "See it is that mentality that they use against us." He made doe eyes and clasped his hands as he continued in a lighter voice, "They can't all be bad. There has to be some good in them." He then continued in his regular voice, "Pah! They are a blight that needs to be exterminated!"

"I'm… sorry you feel that way," Morrigan laughed nervously and wiped her sweaty palms on the bed sheet.

"You should feel the same as I do! They destroyed everything you knew! Friends, family, your way of life!"

"I suppose you make a point…"

Walking to the window, he looked outside, standing with his hands behind his back. "Look, don't think too hard on it. You've been hurt, and once you get over your sadness, I'm sure you'll come to see the world how we see it." He turned, facing Morrigan, "Our road is not an easy one, but it's the right one. I'm not asking you to commit to our cause, but hopefully you'll at least understand that." A few moments of silence passed before a bell rang. "I better get down to report. Get well, and I should be back up later, if you're awake."

"Thank you," Morrigan said softly as Charlie left the room. As soon as the door closed, and she heard Charlie's footsteps go down the hallway she plopped face down on her pillow letting out a muffled scream.

"That wasn't too bad," Verthandi spoke as Morrigan felt her presence seeping into her again.

"Morrigan, are you dragons really that destructive?" Morrigan asked. "Tell me the truth. I want to know for myself."

"No more destructive than the Sentients," Morrigan responded nonchalantly.

Morrigan rolled over on her side, clutching the pillow. "That's not really an answer," she muttered as she curled up around the pillow. "Am I just going to be a puppet in a play? Is it better that I let myself die rather than live a lie knowing that someday I'll bring death and destruction upon some other town, causing the cycle to repeat itself?" She felt her eyes begin to water and the moisture on the pillow, "Katherine seemed as nice as they come, but Gilbert seemed to have a soured past relationship with her. Katherine was pretty mellow when we met, but look at how that turned out? Am I really going to be destined for destruction?" she cried as she buried her face in the pillow.

"You have to remember, Katherine was provoked," Verthandi sighed. "That's like being blamed for killing someone who had been tormenting you all your life."

Morrigan lowered the pillow a little so that her face was no longer buried, "Still, just because I can kill a person, I don't have to. If I can find an example of just one Terrakonan who hasn't destroyed things it would make this pathway so much simpler."

"There are a lot of dragons, all with their own traits and morals," Verthandi said with a heavy exhale. She paused for a bit as she searched for the words to form into a sentence. "Most like the line of logical thinking, which means it's better to eliminate a threat than reason with it. Cost" there was another pause before Verthandi quickly finished off the sentence in one breath, "comes later, and cold as it sounds." There was another pause and a small groan before Verthandi continued, "Sentients don't have the longest of life cycles. For everyone killed by a Terrakonan they have produced four or five. On the other hand, dragon life cycles are long. Kill a dragon and that number is not replaced for *years*. So logically one or two sentients is of little concern to us in the bigger picture."

Morrigan frowned, "That's some cold logic. I mean in the numbers game I see the logic but think about Charlie. That one incident has made him an overzealous dragon hater. Even Katherine snapped when you took the one person that mattered the world to her." She shot up into a sitting position, "Speaking of Katherine, have you talked to her or Nome's dragons? Nome might be dead, but what would that do to Arnhem?" Verthandi did not respond right away and went silent. "What would happen to him? I have to know. Is it really that bad?"

"Do you... remember... the song Katherine was singing that night?"

"The Travelin song?" Morrigan questioned. "Yes? But I don't see what singing has anything to do with—"

"That tells you everything you need to know..."

"I don't get it!"

"The song is called 'Timeless Bonds'. It is a song that warns dragons about getting too attached to their Terrakonans." Morrigan sighed heavily before continuing, "*Before… wandering blind, two souls bind. Towards the light we march until we find ourselves under the timeless arch.* While having a good relationship with a Terrakonans is advantageous, having too strong of a bond causes your souls to bind. Fate suffered by one is suffered by the other…"

"*What!*" Morrigan shrieked. "Is that why you are so adamant that I not kill myself? For your own self-preservation?"

"What? No!" Verthandi bellowed before looking away and speaking in a quieter voice, "No, our spirits aren't bound that tightly yet. If you die, I'd have to find another before my essence runs out in your world. Nome and Arnhem had been together for *centuries*. Their bond is a lot stronger than mine and yours right now."

"Centuries?" Morrigan raised an eyebrow. "Nome doesn't look any older than a quarter century."

"Well, considering a dragon suffers the same fate as their Terrakonan, once the bond goes beyond a certain point, wouldn't it be a good idea to infuse some of the dragon's ageless essence into their Terrakonan?"

"But if you live so much longer than us anyways, why bother at all? If your Terrakonan doesn't live long enough for your souls to bind, you'd have no problem. You've already said you have no problem killing a human or two because they'd simply replace the numbers quickly."

"So, you wouldn't mind if I just took you over and then kept you at a distance, only needing you to peer into your world and for my own means and then discard you when you get old?" Morrigan fell silent. She could not come up with a response. "Exactly. We're not cold-hearted demons as the Rannsoknardomari would have you believe. We are still allowed the same range of feelings and morals as afforded you." There were a few moments of silence before Morrigan spoke.

"I'm sorry," she said softly curling into a ball, eyes watering as she closed them. "I didn't mean to offend, it's just all so new to me and it feels like everything is collapsing around me."

She felt something rub against her cheek. She opened her eyes to see Verthandi standing before her, wiping away her tears with one of her claws.

The clouds had disappeared, and the green field now had some shrubbery growing. There was also a gentle breeze blowing.

"I've not been the most forthcoming partner either so don't cry. I guess we've both got some growing to do. If we're both going to get through this, we'll have to trust each other." Morrigan buried her face in Verthandi's stomach and sobbed. Verthandi tried to resist hugging her, but it lasted only a few moments and she hugged Morrigan back. "Maybe we're all more alike than we'd like to believe," Verthandi whispered as Morrigan fell off to sleep. "Maybe a dose of naivety and idealism is what we all need," she smiled to herself as she looked at a sapling starting to grow from the ground.

. . . .

Morrigan awoke to someone knocking on her door. "Come in," she said, rubbing her head.

Charlie poked his head in, "Oh sorry, were you sleeping?"

"It's ok," she responded rubbing her eyes, "I should probably spend more time awake."

"Good, because I have some food for you from the kitchen," he said as he entered with a tray. The aroma of baked chicken, potatoes and gravy woke her up and she could feel her stomach turning in knots as he approached. She sat up and he rested the tray on a nearby table. He took a napkin out of his pocket and unwrapped two green pills. "The head medic says you should take these to speed up your recovery. You have to eat them before you start eating, you know, just to make sure you aren't too full to take them afterwards. Can't have you overcharging yourself on tablets."

"Okay," Morrigan answered, "but I feel fine, are you sure I need to take them?"

"If the head medic says it's good, it's good. At the very least it won't make you feel any worse," he shrugged. She looked at the pills as he dropped them in her hand and tossed them in her mouth. As her teeth began to sink into the grainy substance of the pill, she felt a sharp pain in her jaw that caused her to wince and she would have shrieked if she had not covered her mouth to keep her from spitting them out.

"Spit it out! Its Gai—" Verthandi yelled, her voice fading away before she could say more. Try as she might, Morrigan was unable to call out or hear anything from Verthandi.

"Is something the matter?" Charlie asked. "Perhaps I should have told you to have some of the drink with the tablet to wash it down instead of having you try to chew it." Morrigan glanced up and saw Charlie taking the cup off the tray and handing it to her. Following Verthandi's last words, she spit the tablets out into her left hand and grabbed the cup with her other hand. Charlie watched her drink the water in the cup, and she handed it back to him.

"Better?" he asked.

"Much," she nodded. She put the tablets under the covers and sat at the edge of the bed while Charlie moved the table closer to the bed for her to eat on.

"Eat what you can, I'll be back in an hour to collect the dishes," he said once the table was in position. He then bowed and left the room. Once she heard his footsteps go down the hallway, she took the pills out from under the covers. They seemed like regular pills. She scratched the green surface and found it was red underneath. She dared not touch it and threw both pills out the window.

"Why would they give her something harmful?" she wondered, half expecting Verthandi to respond, but it never came. She picked at her food, despite being very hungry a few moments earlier; she had now lost her appetite.

Right on cue an hour later Charlie returned to her room. "Not hungry?" he asked, spying about half the meal still on her plate.

"I guess not," she smiled weakly.

"No! Keep them away! You heathens shall pay for that! Even if it costs me my life!" Morrigan heard someone scream down the hall. Charlie quickly stepped all the way into the room and closed the door.

"Is that Gilbert?" Morrigan asked.

"Indeed, it is," Charlie said quietly. "The dragon has taken his mind and plagued it with a never-ending battle. He screams all night long as if he's

50

fighting a war by himself. No matter how far he gets along, he always yells out in pain as he is cut down to size, never all at once, but as if he's being toyed with."

"Do you not have a way to cure it?"

"No, they say it can only be cured once the dragon has been slayed."

"But if we find Katherine and Nome tomorrow, why not just ask them to remove it?"

"I told you before, dragons or Terrakonans can be reasoned with! Even should they consent, it would likely be a move to have us lower our guards so they can kill as many of us before escaping."

"Have you personally tried?"

"No, but why should I? It has been tried before. If someone tells you the fire is hot, do you still touch it? No! It's the logical course of action!"

Morrigan froze at the comment. She forced her mouth shut, "You're... just like them..." she said quietly. "One is no better than the other."

"Look it's good to have your sympathies, but I'll warn you again, don't impede us for we make the hard decisions that those gentler souls cannot."

"I see..." Morrigan said quietly. She then rolled over in her bed, "Well I better get some rest so at least I'll be alert for tomorrow. We are moving early, right?"

"Yes, the crack of dawn," Charlie spoke through his clenched teeth. He took up the tray and left the room, slamming the door shut behind him.

"Could they be onto me?" Morrigan wondered as she curled up in her bed. "Oh Verthandi, where are you when I need you?" Her thoughts were interrupted by a gathering din outside. She carefully got out of bed, lightly placing her feet on the ground before slowly, easing her butt off the bed and shifting her weight to her feet. She held her hands out to her side as she rose up to standing, her mouth agape as she didn't even wobble as she got to a fully standing position. She made her way over to the window, but since there was a light on, she dared not peek out. Instead, she sat down underneath the windowsill and listened intently.

"Tomorrow men, we trap a Terrakonan! You are not to let their youthful appearance fool you, nor should you let it be used against you! Gird yourself strong. Remember this is for a better world, for your fellow man, that they would no longer have to contend with the taint of the Terrakonans!" Morrigan heard the voice. Although it sounded familiar she was unable to verify the identity of the speaker. She wanted badly to look over the top to see, but at the same time she did not want to give the impression that she was spying. Those gathered let out a loud cheer before breaking out in song.

From our perch we stand, gazing down on the world.

To see the endless taint of the wyrm.

Black with hatred and conquest the darkness threatens.

The bold picked up weapons to fight! And the war was on.

Their lives remembered in valiant song.

And like rain the dragons shall fall.

Their blood trickles down our blades. Their blood trickles down to the grave. Their blood will flow until it sates our ancestor's vengeance.

And then we will stand on Earth born anew. Glorious and free of their taint.

Until then, the war shall rage on! The bold will fight on.

Until there is nothing left of their existence but an echo of song.

As they were finishing the song, Morrigan heard footsteps approaching her room. She scrambled back to her bed and quickly pretended to be asleep. She heard the door creak open and heard Charlie speak quietly, "Yes, she's asleep."

"Good," another voice responded. "We don't know how she survived Katherine's wrath, perhaps it was a fluke, but at the very least she doesn't show any signs of withdrawal or part of her being missing."

"Maybe she's a new Terrakonan which would explain her survival and lack of a response."

"Unlikely. After all, Terrakonans are trained for their responsibility from a young age. Remember that convent we destroyed? They are bred, trained, indoctrinated into believing there is no other life than to serve a dragon. That way once the bond is formed, they are unable to live without it."

"Point taken," Charlie said as he closed the door back shut. The conversation continued outside, but Morrigan was unable to hear it.

"Withdrawal? What do they mean… withdrawal?" Morrigan thought aloud. As she did, she felt a sharp pain in her chest, like someone had stabbed her. The pain travelled up her body to her head and she whited out into another place.

The place she came to was in a charred landscape. The ground was still smouldering, littered with an assortment of weapons as well as dead bodies, both sentient and dragons of various sizes. The sky was a clear purple hue Morrigan assumed was from the constant lightning bouncing between all the dust and smoke clouds. The smell of burnt meat and cloth permeated everything. She then became aware of someone letting out a heavy sigh. Turning to face the sigh, she saw a woman dressed in a pastel pink loose skirt that was about midway down her thigh, with a matching short sleeved shirt and flats. A long black scabbard was on the right side of her hip. Her light red hair was tied back into a loose ponytail, held in place with a black bow.

"I don't know why she insists on being so tsundere with everything...." she muttered as she put her hands on her hips and shook her head.

"Um, excuse me?"

Before Morrigan could say anymore, the woman had drawn her blade and Morrigan felt its cold steel against her neck despite it having a fiery glow to it. "Oh, it's you," the woman relented after a moment as her features softened.

"What is with that response?" Morrigan breathed a little easier as the woman withdrew the sword. "I don't even know where I am!"

"Was it that traumatic that you don't remember what you set in motion? Granted it is a surprise to see you around these parts. I thought you had already become dust in the wind," the woman said as she rubbed the sides of her head and closed her eyes. "I'm not one to normally see spirits, but I will indulge you as you have made my friend exceedingly disappointed with this ending."

"One week ago, you delivered Nome to the Rannsoknardomari. They made a public spectacle of her execution, sending her sister into a soul shattering fury. With the souls of Arnhem and Nogomain the Heavenly Dragons were able to open the gate between Tumahab and Terra. Dragons, sensing their time had come to exact vengeance for their separation from their beloved Terrakonans for so long poured through the gate. The resulting fight is the carnage you see before you."

Morrigan felt another stab in her chest and her heartbeat seemed to almost resonate in her head and she went down to one knee and whited out again. When her sight returned, she found herself back in the stone walls of the Rannsoknardomari room. Her breathing was very quick and heavy, as was her heart rate.

"What was that?" Morrigan wondered. "A charred world after handing over Nome. But Nome is already dead. And Katherine has already retaliated. If I'm to believe Charlie, so long as Katherine lives, Gilbert remains under her spell. But if she's still alive, does that mean she comes back to finish me off?"

She rolled over on her back to look at the ceiling, as her right hand spread across her forehead., "What even was that I saw? The future? But…" She then shot up out of bed, "Oh *crap*! Tomorrow at the library. It's a trap. The tablet was meant to separate me from my dragon in the event I was Terrakonan. That means I'd have nothing to resist them with at the library. I'll meet Nome tomorrow at the library and…"

She quickly got out of bed and ran over to the door. She then recalled how she was able to hear everyone's footsteps and figured that might not be the best way to go if she wanted to get out undetected. She then ran over to the window and saw she was in a second-floor room. Jumping from so high might hurt herself, or the landing would create noise. She peered out the window and saw ledges but was unsure if she could escape via those. She looked back to the bed and got the idea of tying the bed sheets together. She quickly tied the top sheet and the bottom sheet together before tying it off on the bedpost. It did not get her all the way to the bottom, but it was closer than jumping from the second floor. She began her descent down the sheets. As she slowly made her way down, she heard a noise and stopped to listen. She looked up and saw the sheet pulling taught over the windowsill and was starting to rip. She tried to move a little faster, but the sheets ripped completely before she reached the end of the rope. She landed initially on her feet, but the shock was jarring enough that she fell backwards on her butt. The sheet landed around and on top of her. She took a few moments to make sure she had feeling in her feet before darting off towards the exit gate. The first rays of light were beginning to show on the dark sky as she darted out of the gate.

Chapter 9

It took her a while to locate the library as she had to stop and ask for directions. By the time she got there, she was out of breath. She took a few minutes leaning over her knees, taking in big breaths in rapid succession before going in. "No! I need to find Nome!" she thought, pulling herself together as she went inside still breathing heavily.

The library was larger than she'd ever imagined. There were shelves spiralling up multiple floors as well as arched and alleyways formed by arrangements of books. Several shelves went up multiple floors, some being split by pathways and ladders that seemed to be around every corner.

"She could be *anywhere*!" Morrigan thought to herself as she began systematically going down the various pathways, looking in all the nooks and crannies of the library. Even the smallest of spaces, Morrigan peered into just to make sure no one was there before hastily moving on to the next area. Her temperature and heart rate rose as the minutes ticked by looking for Nome.

Finally, after what seemed like an eternity, she found her perched on a small ladder in a far corner of the library with a large brown book on her lap. At first Morrigan could only see the cover illustration of some winged person in white and blue holding a shiny object in their hands over their head. She got a little closer and saw the titles as *Draconic Myths and Legends*.

As she was about to speak, Nome spoke first, "You have the *nerve* to come here," she hissed.

"Nome, I'm really sorry about what happened before, but you have to listen to me!" Morrigan said, trying not to yell as she stopped at the foot of the ladder.

"Why should I?" Nome's eyes narrowed. "Because you didn't want to help, Kat is on the brink of literally bursting. I thought she might have killed you, but obviously now that isn't the case." She slammed her book shut between her two hands, "Even if you are a Terrakonan, all you do is cause trouble to us. Kat should have just let me kill you before you got too far, or maybe we should have just left you to the elements."

"Nome! I've got no time for semantics; the Rannsoknardomari will be here any minute to kill you. They know you're here."

"And who *told* them that?" Nome fired back.

Morrigan went quiet for a moment. Her fists clenched and she looked at the ground, before looking back up to Nome. "I did. I told them…" she said softly.

"Hmph," Nome huffed as she climbed down from the ladder. She glared at Morrigan as she reached the bottom for a few moments. Morrigan could feel her hair standing on edge for those few moments, before Nome turned away. "Thanks, I guess," Nome mumbled.

"I'm sorry," Morrigan whispered.

"Don't be!" a voice yelled from behind Morrigan. Morrigan spun around to face the voice and saw Charlie.

"It had to be you didn't it," Nome sneered.

"Nome Mamoragan, by the powers vested in me by the Rannsoknardomari, I hereby arrest you for the murder and destruction of the villages of Mokey and Gelaba!"

"Gelaba?" Nome did a double take.

Morrigan then jumped between the two, "Nome did not kill at Gelaba. There was a dragon present for that, a large golden dragon with blue eyes. It morphed into a man with golden hair, blue eyes and gold armour."

Nome seemed to snap up at the description and said something, but it was inaudible.

"One town less, it still doesn't matter, she and her sister are still responsible for Mokey, and even if she is not here, we know that she will come out once we put Nome in danger," he said with a wicked smile.

"Prepare yourself then, for I will not allow myself to be captured again without resistance," Nome said as her eyes took on a golden hue. Her fingers extended themselves with lightning to become large electrical claws. "Step aside Morrigan, I will fight to the death, if need be, to escape. I will not give up nor surrender." Pushing Morrigan out of the way, her claws came together to form a blade on each hand. She then crossed the blades in front of her face, "Charlie Derby, you have threatened my life. As such you have nullified my promise to Mio."

"Silence! You have no right to call on her name after you slaughtered her! Men! Seize them!" he ordered.

"If only you knew…" Nome sighed as the soldiers ran around Charlie to attack Nome. Morrigan felt another sharp pain in her chest and a loud thump in her head. Her sight whited out and she reappeared in what looked like a village.

Five people, two females and three males, were sitting in a wooden house. The two young boys looked like Gilbert and Charlie. One of the two of the girls was Katherine. Morrigan was unsure on the identity of the other girl, but she had the prettiest blonde hair and blue eyes she had ever seen and also appeared to be roughly the same age as Katherine. The last man was old, covered in an unusual type of clothing that hid his figure, but his hands were thin and bony. What little she could see of his skin was wrinkly.

They were sitting in a circle, with two crystals, one blue and one black, lying in between them. Everyone was sitting cross legged, eyes closed and arms out to their sides. The old man's lips were moving while the unknown girl had opened her eyes, starting to reach out to the black crystal.

Charlie, who was sitting next to her, tried to stop it, and wound up knocking it out of her hand. It rolled across the circle to Katherine. At this point it seemed Katherine smiled and nodded, and the crystal leapt from the ground trying to bury itself into her chest.

The girl and Charlie froze with shock and fear as Katherine winced in pain and struggled to hold her position before doubling over in pain. They both neglected to notice the other blue crystal as it fused with the unknown girl. Charlie looked as if he screamed out "Mio" as both the girls fell to the ground meanwhile the hazy figure of a black dragon appeared over the old man.

The boys tried to prevent the last bit of the crystal from sinking into her chest but to no avail. There was a large flash and the vision faded away. With a deep inhale she returned to the library.

"What happened Nome? All that flash and pomp was just for show?" Charlie jeered. Nome's blades had begun to dim and were not as bright as they were before. Her posture was not steady and was showing signs of going lax, breathing heavily. There were blood splatters and dead bodies all around her. The patrons who were in the library were running outside, screaming. "I must applaud you for outstripping my healing, but now your energy is waning. Your dragon just as in history has abandoned you in your hour of need."

"Avalanche!" Morrigan yelled out. Both combatants looked upwards but saw nothing. However, Nome refocused back below faster and sliced through the base of the shelves to her left and right, causing the towering shelves to collapse inward, cascading thousands of books on top of them. Morrigan curled up and raised her hands over her head to protect it from the falling books. She saw a flash and Nome was gone.

"Dammit!" Charlie screamed as he saw Nome had escaped. He then marched over to Morrigan and grabbed her by the hair. "You! Traitor!" he yelled as he lifted her out of the books that had piled around her. "I told you not to interfere with our work!"

"I couldn't let you just kill her," Morrigan winced as she quickly stood on her feet to alleviate the weight on her hair.

"That is *not* for you to decide!" he yelled. "Now we have a pile of dead men and women who died because you *warned* a Terrakonan and then aided in her escape. Now you'll have to take her place in execution!" Morrigan then felt something hit her hard against her head and she blacked out.

Chapter 10

When she came to, she felt a shiver as the cold breeze was blowing. Opening her eyes, as far as the eyes could see there was a sea of trees. "Welcome back," Charlie sneered, "although I don't know for how long." Morrigan tried to move her hands but found them restrained behind her. "Don't worry, those bindings are pretty tight," Charlie jeered. "But due to crimes committed against the Rannsoknardomari, you will be tried as a Terrakonan. You will be thrown off this cliff. If you are truly a human you will die on the ground below, but if you're a Terrakonan, you will attempt to fly away." He then pointed above him and Morrigan followed his finger to a giant ballista on the ledge above them. "You will be impaled by that should you even make an attempt to fly."

"That's not a very fair trial," Morrigan snapped.

"It's not very fair that you allowed a Terrakonan to escape to wreak havoc another day."

"Oh, that stuff *finally* wore off!" Morrigan heard Verthandi echo in her mind.

"You have some really bad timing…" Morrigan responded.

"Oh my, the Terrakonan trial," Verthandi responded after getting a quick glance around. "Just save them the trouble and jump."

"Are you *crazy*? I can't fly."

"We've never tried, but you're dead regardless, and by the time you power up standing right in front of a squadron *and* a ballista, you'd be dead if we tried something on the top here."

"Any last words traitor?" Charlie interrupted the conversation.

"Charlie, what if I told you your friend is not dead? Nor was Nome responsible for the disaster that destroyed your village."

"I'd say you're lying and merely stalling your execution."

"It's true though! Your village elder tricked you. You've been deceived!"

"Throw her over! Before I have to kill her myself for trying to sway my mind! My mind is fortified; no simple tricks will deceive it!" Before she could say anything else, she was grabbed and thrown over.

"So this is how it ends?" Morrigan thought. She felt an itching sensation on her back contorted her body to try to soothe the irritation.

"Keep still, will you?" Verthandi echoed.

"There is something bothering my back, it's like the world doesn't even want me to die in peace."

"Relax, I'm trying to give you wings, but you have to trust me. Don't resist anything. We don't have a lot of time nor margin for error. That ballista is trained on you if we're to pull this off I need complete control just above the tree line. Trust me."

The ground continued screaming towards Morrigan for a few seconds before she clasped her hands and closed her eyes. "Okay, I trust you. Keep us safe." Morrigan felt the itching sensation give way to almost something ripping out of her back. She winced at the new sensation, but it was soon smoothed over. She felt her velocity slow a little before something whizzed by as she felt her body roll over to the side and hearing a metallic clank. She felt her feet graze some branches and leaves before feeling her body lift upwards.

"I've forgotten how awkward it is to fly another," Verthandi mused as Morrigan opened her eyes to see her feet dangling just above the treetops.

"We're really flying!" Morrigan gasped as she looked down to see the canopy below her.

"Don't rock the boat too much; I'm just barely keeping this. I need to show you how to properly control and steer before we can do anything like reaching out to things."

"Oh, ok," Morrigan said as she brought her arms back close to her body. She then added quietly, "Thank you."

"Think nothing of it, although you may want to reconsider before back talking to another member of the Rannsoknardomari again."

"Oh!" Morrigan exclaimed as she tried to straighten out her posture, causing herself to lose altitude before Verthandi was able to recover, preventing them from crashing into the canopy. "Sorry, sorry," Morrigan said sheepishly, "But something happened that was really... strange."

"Oh?"

"I was having these pains in my chest and then whiting out to random events. Once in the past, it was black and white I couldn't interact with anyone. The other was a future where there was just one person there and I was able to talk to them."

"I guess more of me stayed behind and has been fusing with you than I'd like. I'm a seer dragon. I can see things past, present and future. Although I can see things, I seem to have trouble picking up things with my Terrakonans." Verthandi paused for a brief second before continuing. "I can't tell them when something will be dangerous or the outcome of it, granted I can't see things directly with me either. However, you are the first Terrakonan I've had who inherited the skill. Not even those trained to be my Terrakonans had ever been able to see flashbacks of those around them." She scratched her head with a single claw, "Sadly, it isn't a skill you can generally control. The visions tend to be fairly random, and they incapacitate you when you see them."

"I see..." Morrigan sighed.

"What did you see? In the past?"

"I saw Nome, Katherine, Gilbert and Charlie as friends. They had another girl with them and an old man. It looked like they were doing a ritual with what I assume to be dragon crystals. Katherine and the mystery girl both absorbed one crystal, while the old man seemed to emanate a shadow dragon. The house exploded shortly afterwards, and I was out of the vision."

"Hmmm, that could be both a good and a bad thing…" Verthandi mused.

"In what way?"

"Well, the good part is you know what happened, even if the other five present do not. The bad part is, for that to be true, Gilbert and Charlie would have had to find some way to live until around eight hundred years."

"Eight… *hundred!*" Morrigan jumped causing Verthandi to once again lose some control before righting the flight path again. "Sorry, it's just, eight hundred years when none of them look over twenty-five."

"In your terms, eight hundred is a large number, but to us it is around middle age and not surprising. Nogomain for instance is nearly one thousand and Arnhem is around seven hundred."

"How old are you?" Morrigan asked quietly.

"Old, over one thousand," Verthandi laughed a little.

"Woooww" Morrigan responded before quickly adding, "You look good for your age."

"Ha! I care not for your vanities," Verthandi laughed, "but your thoughts are appreciated." She then added in a grave tone, "But you bring up a valid point, for Gilbert and Charlie to have been alive for so long they themselves are either Terrakonans or there is some other magic at work."

"Any ideas? The Terrakonan idea is probably the best, but it would really be stupid to be working for an anti-Terrakonan organization all this time and no one has noticed."

"Yet in your vision of the future, you said all was razed, meaning the Rannsoknardomari had been wiped out as well. It is possible there could be possible Terrakonans within them; however, for ones to be there for so long would be pushing the boundaries of belief."

"But if there are sufficient numbers to hide the rebellious numbers then it could be feasible, they are all hiding in plain sight and waiting for a signal."

"I know who would have a better idea," Verthandi said as she veered northward. "I know who might have a better idea…."

Chapter 11

"How do you know all these Terrakonans?"

"It's no secret who does and doesn't have Terrakonans in Tumahab. The problem is being able to locate them, since most Terrakonans are forced to be nomadic. A combination of sentients, particularly the Rannsoknardomari, not trusting them and sometimes Tumahab politics spills over and assassinations happen. However, these two almost *never* move."

"Maybe they're that confident in their abilities."

"No, nothing like that... just you'll see when we get there. In the meantime, tell me more about these visions you saw." Morrigan proceeded to tell Verthandi about the visions she had seen in better detail, only stopping when she felt a chill in the air.

"Brr, it's cold up here," Morrigan shivered.

"This is one of the reasons these two never move," Verthandi responded. "We'll have to go the rest of the way on foot before the snow and ice comes. Now keep your feet up and lean back, we're going to attempt a landing."

"What is up? And how do you lean back?"

"If your feet are in front of you and hit the ground first you hit the ground running enough to prevent falling over face first. You should be leaning back as a result of impact, but you will move forward for a few paces." Morrigan put up her feet as instructed; however, she brought her feet up too high and instead of running slid out and landed on her butt.

"Not bad for a first attempt," Verthandi snorted. "Legs a little lower next time, you're not bracing for impact, you're preparing to hit the ground running."

"Oh, ok," Morrigan responded, rising to her feet, retracting her wings into her back. As she started to walk a strong gust of wind blew, stopping Morrigan in her tracks. "It's *freezing*!" Morrigan said as she shivered, rubbing her hands up and down her arms.

"Right, have some smouldering scales. They should keep you warm for now." Morrigan was about to question Verthandi when she felt her skin get tight. It then morphed in small scales that changed the hue of her skin to a faint burnt sienna colour. She let out a content sigh as she felt the warmth seep into her body. "Better?"

"Much better," Morrigan responded. Soon she came to the entrance of a cave, just below the snow line. Verthandi indicated they should proceed in. It was dank and dark, even with Verthandi's improved sight; it was hard to see anything in the cave. Fortunately, the cave was a very straight path until it opened up into a large room. In the middle were the glowing embers from a small campfire.

"Are you *sure* they don't move?" Morrigan asked as she approached the campfire and looked around. "The fire does look recent, but it would appear no one is here, and we didn't pass anyone on the way in."

"Oh, it's you," they heard a yawn from the entrance to the room. Morrigan turned around quickly to face the voice but saw nothing other than a blanket of cold air spreading along the ground. "I didn't think the rumours were true when they said Verthandi managed to get her old Terrakonan killed and pick up another one so quickly." She felt something cold, dead cold rest on her shoulder. Morrigan shrieked and jumped away from where she was and turned to see a small dragonling hovering next to where she was standing. "Oh-ho, one with good reflexes," the little dragon laughed as it rolled around in mid-air.

"Not funny!" Morrigan fired off.

"Oh, but it is, you are not dead, and I am amused, but where are my manners?" The cold air blanket began travelling up to the little dragon and forming ice crystals. The ice crystals first attached themselves to its wings, giving it a feathery appearance before filling in as a human body standing around one hundred and seventy-five centimetres tall.

Once the air blanket was consumed the layer of ice exploded revealing a man with short cut straight blue hair with white tips and black eyes. His wings maintained their feathery sheen, which contrasted with his tan complexion. "My name is Chimalli, Terrakonan to Itztlacoliuhqui, or as I call him Itzl for short," he said with an exaggerated bow. "And I take it you are Verthandi's new Terrakonan."

"Indeed, I am," Morrigan nodded.

"So new, Verthandi hasn't taught you etiquette. For shame Verthandi, for shame." He then returned to a standing position. "Regardless, we can refine you at a later date since I assume you are not here for tea and biscuits." He snapped his fingers and Morrigan felt the ground rumble before hearing a deafening roar as the cave they entered through became blocked with snow and debris. Just as she was about to complain about being blocked in, one of the far walls behind him crumbled away, revealing a lit pathway. "This way," he motioned down the path that opened up.

Morrigan hesitated for a brief moment before following Chimalli down the pathway. At the end of the pathway was a painting of what looked like a park in a city. There were people running about, some with wings, and some without on a green field. A lake was in the upper left with a dragon ferrying little children to a dock, and in the blue skies above there were people riding on dragons.

"What is that?" Morrigan asked.

"It is a picture of the original Asteria, painted long before any of us were around. A time and place where dragon and humans lived side by side." He touched the painting and ripples formed. At first Morrigan thought she was seeing things, but the objects began to move. The dragons flew out of the field of vision, and the children were jumping off the dragon in the water and climbing back on.

The people both winged and non-winged were laughing and playing with each other. "A time we've tried to recreate. That being said, if you do not believe that humans and dragons can live in harmony, please do not express those views here. We pride ourselves on our unity and harmony." He then stepped through the painting, reappearing as part of the picture a short time later.

Morrigan swallowed hard and followed suit. In a flash she found herself in the middle of a park. The air was fresh and clear. The sound of laughter seemed to be the dominant sound. She looked around and everyone seemed happy. The children were playing; the adults were discussing things, even a dragon that was running a nearby ice cream cart seemed to happily be discussing things with his customers. And standing next to her was Verthandi. She was not quite as large as when they met in Ardivian Space, and was actually closer to Morrigan's own size, maybe a head or two taller. Morrigan and Verthandi looked at each other for a few seconds before slowly reaching out their hands to one another.

"How?" They both echoed in unison as they turned to face Chimalli, who was now standing next to a blue dragon that stood a little taller than him, on all fours.

"Welcome to Neo Assssteria. Originally named for Assssteria of old, we also ssssit on the Assssterian Gate, which we were charged to protect aeons ago," the blue dragon spoke. "While protecting, we figured a town would be good if only to show both dragonsss and ssssentientsss that we can live together as we onccccce did."

"Wow…" Morrigan marvelled as she looked around.

"While it's all fine and dandy here, do they ever leave here?" Verthandi asked.

"Of course, they do," Chimalli chuckled. "Even my own kids have left here. Some come back, some don't. Sometimes they bring back friends."

"And *everyone* is a believer?" Morrigan asked.

"No, not everyone. We've had a few… casssses we've had to deal with. On both sssssidessss. Sssssssometimessss we get problem dragonssssss, ssssometimesss we get problem ssssssentientsss. It issss how life worksssss," Itzl said.

"But what happens if one of those disgruntled ones brings back either the slayers or more dragons?"

"Well firstly, you can only come in through the human side of the gate. This means the only dragons entering are entering via their Terrakonans. Secondly, the slayers can't open it as you need some form of dragon essence to open the gate through the painting. So, unless they are gathering up dragon essence or recruiting Terrakonans, it's unlikely for them to get here," Chimalli said, holding up two fingers.

"Actually, funny you should mention that. That is one of the reasons we are here," Morrigan said. Chimalli and Itzl looked at each other. "I'm being serious! There are two people in the Rannsoknardomari who have apparently lived as long as Terrakonans which is well over a few centuries!"

"That isss indeed troubling," Itzl hissed. "Perhapsss we should conssssult Ccccitlacue."

"Sounds good." Chimalli then spoke to Verthandi and Morrigan, "We're going to have to stop off at the Babbling Brook, Citlacue and her Terrakonan Tozi like to entertain with song."

Chapter 12

The group left the park and Morrigan and Verthandi both marvelled at what they saw. Dragons and humans both travelled along the roads and the skies with neither seeming particularly bothered by the other. There were conversations, a nursery, street vendors, farmers and gardeners, all working together. At one point they heard a dragon and a human arguing, but as it turned out, they were both making sarcastic jabs at something they had overheard in the outside world, and they resolved their conflict with a rousing laugh.

Smells came and went; the dragons flying overhead seemed to have an effect of keeping the air moving and no one smell dominated the others. There were no vehicles of any sort, except for the occasional cart which generally was drawn by whomever the operator was. Mass transit seemed to be carried out by dragons, but as Chimalli pointed out, their human Terrakonans rode along with them, if only to keep them company on some of the quieter routes. Eventually, the group found themselves in front of a large blue wooden building. The smell of smoke and alcohol hit them like a wall as they opened the front door and entered.

The building seemed bigger on the inside as even some of the larger dragons were seated at tables talking and laughing with each other and humans. There was an area in the far side of the building which had higher chairs and tables for groups of the larger dragons. There was a weird smell on the smoke, and they saw some of the dragons burning what looked like different coloured plants. In the centre of the room was a stage and a blue dragon similar in form and size to Itzl sat in a chair with a lute while next to her was a human with black hair in a bun and wearing a huipil and long skirt which were dark blue with a light blue dragon that went across the front of the huipil holding a small ukulele.

"Alright guys and gals, I know you're all having a good time, but our next song is going to be Kronos' Lament. A dragon who found his love, but lost her again after spending too much time ignoring her. So, remember everything in moderation, even fun and don't forget to spend time with your loved ones," the woman announced as she and the dragon slowed the tempo of their strumming. They then proceeded to sing alternate lines of the song.

Find me still searching.

For the one who loved me.

Searching still seeking

To quench the flame inside me

Promise to survive

Until we are united once more

Fire Eternal

Burning Infernal

Gone are the days so joyful

Even with work they're mournful

And so I sleep waiting for that day

O happy day

When we can enjoy the twilight

Of a blissful silent night.

The crowd loudly applauded once the song was completed and both dragon and human did a polite curtsy before leaving the stage after spying Chimalli and Itzl in the crowd.

"It must be serious if you're here and not junior," the woman frowned as she stood next to Chimalli.

"Indeed, it is Tozi," he stepped aside, pushing Morrigan in front of him. "This is Morrigan, she's Verthandi's Terrakonan."

"How do you do," Tozi said with a smile and a small curtsy.

"They are here because they are concerned that there may be Terrakonans who may be starting to infiltrate the Rannsoknardomari."

Tozi's smile melted into a frown, and she tilted her head slightly to the side, "If true that is indeed very bad news." She stated looking at Morrigan, "But what proof do you have to support such a claim?"

"I've run into two other Terrakonans; Nome and Katherine. They seemed to have relations with two others who I came across when I was with the Rannsoknardomari. Further to that I saw a vision of all four gathered as children when I assumed Katherine inherited her dragon stone."

"An interesting tale to be sure, except for this dragon stone." She looked at Citlacue, "We don't usually bind with dragon stones, but it might also be interesting to locate either this other child or the old man. While your vision does provide some detail, there are others that don't add up, like, why bring in five kids for only two stones?"

"We can assume the witnesses were to draw hatred towards dragons and Terrakonans. However, for someone to plan that far in advance would be a monumental plan. Someone who thinks really long term. Someone who would already know that all five would live for a very long time," Citlacue mused.

"So, another dragon?" Morrigan asked.

"More than likely," Citlacue nodded. "Alternatively, it could be another Terrakonan."

"But why would a Terrakonan cause an incident that just draws more hatred towards them?" Verthandi asked.

"There is an entire litany of answers to that question. Most revolve around the original reasons the dragons were banished in the first place."

Just then the crowd erupted into cheers and whistles as another singer came to the stage. She had golden eyes and a light brown complexion, with a dazzling smile. Her hair was jet black, but the tips were a similar shade of golden as her eyes.

"Thank you all for your warm support," they could barely hear her speaking over the din. "I'm going to perform one of your favourites," she said as the crowd quieted down. They then broke back out into cheers as she held the first syllable of the song.

O Mighty See

Why can't you see

I want to be free

Free to ride the winds of change

Free to not be choosy of whom I engage

O Mighty See

Why can't you let me be

A traditional relic of the past

Leaving us aghast

Shame on you for deceiving

Shame on us for believing

That you could see all

When you had lost your powers to recall

A bloody past

That you turned into a jest

Having us believe we were best

But truly no different than the rest

Tozi and Citlacue both looked at each other as he sang the refrain again. "The Dragon Seers," they echoed in unison looking at Verthandi.

"What are those looks for? I don't have anything to do with this," Verthandi said, raising her hands.

"No, it's not what you did, it's what you didn't do," Citlacue responded. "Your partner has seen a vision, but have you seen it?"

"No," Verthandi said in a muffled tone, lowering her head.

"But she is a seer though, right?" Morrigan asked.

"She is, but she hasn't actually seen anything for *centuries*," Citlacue responded. "None of the seers have, and neither have their Terrakonans. You are the first in a long time to show signs of the old seers, unrefined as the skill may be. Are you sure *you're* not the fifth child?"

"No," Morrigan grimaced. "I've never met any of the other four a day in my life, nor do I remember anything about seeing a dragon before all this started. I was forcibly fused with Verthandi after finding her old Terrakonan!"

"Speaking of which, Verthandi, what happened to your old Terrakonan?" Tozi interrupted.

"He was ambushed and killed by a gold dragon. We narrowly escaped to Morrigan's town, and we found her on the outskirts of town. We did a quick transfer before without any thought."

"How do you know it was a gold dragon?"

"We saw it! A gold dragon! With two dragonlings!"

"See, information like that would be useful earlier. That means there is an actual dragon on the human side of the divide. And a *breeding* dragon at that if there are dragonlings. But I have another concern. If this dragon was so determined to kill your last Terrakonan, why has it not pursued your current one?"

74

"It obviously thinks my Terrakonan is dead," Verthandi replied almost instantly with a shrug.

Citlacue scowled at Verthandi, "Come now, even you can't be going to fool yourself with such a lie, and neither am I that simple to believe it either."

"But I have not sensed any nearby dragons lately," Verthandi responded.

"It had to be close enough to have ambushed your old Terrakonan, so obviously it has figured a way to mask itself. While it is possible that upon the initial transfer, he might have missed the energy signature, it's highly unlikely they would have dismissed the energy for over a week."

"Regardless, it would appear there is at least one dragon on this side who wants to eliminate the other dragons' presence."

Chimalli then interrupted the conversation, "I hate to break up your train of thought, but if this dragon had it out for Verthandi, I'm sure it had to realise a second Terrakonan rose up to take the place of its predecessor. And from that, it's possible to deduce that she may have been followed here or to our doorstep at the very least."

"But one dragon shouldn't make a threat to a society such as this," Morrigan remarked.

"Have you not been listening to this conversation?" Tozi frowned. "There is a *breeding* gold dragon. We have no idea how much breeding has taken place. Additionally, we have no idea if the dragon is in league with the Rannsoknardomari, and if it has clout in there, they could march here, and we'd be overrun."

"Even with all these dragons?" Morrigan asked.

Citlacue frowned, "The vast majority of the dragons here do not have a fighting edge. Yes, they have some instincts, but instincts versus a finely tuned fighting force will only get you so far." Looking out towards the crowd, Citlacue looked to see who was now singing another song along with the person on the stage, "This town was built on trust and friendship. You see how you entered, and none judged you or looked at you strangely? That's the type of trust and freedom we're all given here. If they ever got in here, by the time the people here realise it's an invasion, it would already be too late."

"So, you're just going to wait for the inevitable?" Verthandi asked.

Citlacue turned to refocus back on the group, "No. We can move the town to the other side of the divide."

"The other side?" Morrigan and Verthandi said in unison.

"Did you not remember what we told you at the ssstart of thissss conversssssation?" Itzl hissed. "We sssit on the Asssterian Gate. We can activate them and move the entire town through the gate to the Tumahab ssside asss a temporary measssure."

"But if you activate the gate, couldn't they just follow you through?"

"No silly, we'll close it behind us. Unless they have an ancient dragon with them or possibly the gold dragon that attacked you it's highly unlikely, they'd know how to operate the gate," Chimalli responded. "And if they do activate it, we'd get a heads up and be able to intercept them during transport."

"But what if their dragon counterpart is on the other side waiting for you?" Morrigan asked.

Chimali nodded, "Just like we're sheltered on this side, we'd still be sheltered on the other side. A dragon on its own cannot enter the town. It has to be the combined essence found in a Terrakonan. Don't worry so much, we move from time to time as a safety measure so that we're never in the same place long should any would-be enemies or even accidental adventurers find us." she then took a step forward, turning slightly away from them, "Well let's get this started, since we don't know our time frame. We'll notify the inn to open up two rooms for you, since as a general rule we don't like to have people present when we initiate the transport process." Morrigan and Verthandi nodded and Chimalli gave them directions to the inn.

"Oh, if you two want to brave the sky roads, stay on the left. As we tell the other new people, left is right, and right is wrong. They do take some getting used to though and seeing as we're about to go on emergency lockdown you probably wouldn't want to be caught out," Chimalli said before bidding them farewell. He hopped on Itzl while Morrigan and Verthandi watched them ascend far above the buildings into the stream of flying dragons above.

"So this is what it was like back in the beginning?" Morrigan asked Verthandi as they began walking towards the inn.

"Very much so," Verthandi nodded. "If I had not witnessed this myself, I'd have said that such a place could never again exist."

"But we get along... fine. Katherine and Nogomain get along fine and even Nome and Arnhem didn't seem to show any distrust between each other."

"A handful does not account for everyone. Think of the dragon that attacked your village. Now imagine those sentients who have similar violent ambitions." Verthandi paused briefly to watch Morrigan's reaction. Morrigan gave a slow nod before Verthandi continued, "Just because two are compatible doesn't make them productive. There are some who would join forces in an alliance to further their own means. There are some who would join out of convenience." She then added in a sharper tone looking directly at Morrigan, "Even you, would you have done this if asked? Probably not. The thing is that they have an entire society built on the friendship and evenness of both dragon and sentient.

"So, what *did* actually happen between the dragons and humans that we've become so divided? You've never told me the story, even though you appear to be one of the oldest dragons around." Verthandi fell silent, her head hung low, looking at the ground. Morrigan then repeated the question again. Verthandi stopped walking. Looking at Morrigan briefly, she let out a long sigh.

"Like you, one of the last visions we saw was that of a scorched world. However, no one could pinpoint the exact reasoning behind it. The sentients blamed the dragons as they had the obvious natural power to do it, while the dragons pinned the blame on the sentients saying they were above such trivial destruction." She paused, looking up at the sky as her claws hung to her sides before looking back at Morrigan, "Tensions rose as one side blamed the other; still others worked together to try and find the true answer. Sentients, being sentients, developed a weapon called the dragon slayer. The dragon population plummeted after that, and the dwindling numbers then took their rage out on the sentients."

"In blind rage they destroyed guilty and innocents alike. It was then decided the seers had seen the demise of the dragons, not the destruction of the world. In one final action we separated the dragons and humans by a mystical barrier. This then led to unrest as dragons on good terms with sentients felt betrayed and demanded some link to be restored. We took pity on them and created the link we now call Terrakonans. This shift caused the last few believers to take power away from the Seers and allowed for the Council of Ta'lel to be formed. There were those who believed that the sentients caused the destruction of our harmonious co-existence and blamed the Seers for misleading the populace."

"So you blame yourself for what happened?" Morrigan asked quietly.

"Largely, yes. And as the last of the seers, it's a large burden to carry..."

Morrigan hugged Verthandi, "Don't worry, I don't blame you for anything. Just like you couldn't stop that disaster, I couldn't stop the destruction of my town. Even if it was partially my own doing having taken over from your previous Terrakonan. We're now in this together. Perhaps now we can help avert this next disaster from happening."

"Maybe..." Verthandi responded wistfully. "Maybe..."

"Population of Neo Asteria, we have received reports of potential danger to our town and are preparing a shift. Please report indoors until advised when the shift is complete. Thank you for your cooperation," Tozi's voice echoed through the city.

"We better get moving to the inn," Morrigan said as she broke off the embrace. "Since we don't know what will happen if we aren't indoors." Verthandi nodded as they quickly made their way to the inn.

By the time they got to the inn the once bustling roads and parks were empty, as was the skies above them. There was nothing outside, except for a few stragglers and the wind.

"You must be the outsiders I was told about!" a man spoke as they entered the inn. His voice was loud and boisterous and the laugh he let out seemed to resonate so strong it shook the room they were in.

"Yes, we are," Morrigan spoke with a nervous laugh.

"There is no need to be afraid! Welcome to Faraway Castle, where Me Casa is Su Casa."

"Now, now dear, there is no need to frighten them." Morrigan screamed and stumbled back towards Verthandi as a nearby dragon statue blinked and began to move.

"Now who's scaring them!" the man said with another hearty laugh.

"Oh, sorry, I didn't know you were actually *alive*," Morrigan huffed, clutching her chest.

"I'm sorry; I didn't mean to frighten you. I zone out during these shifts, since chances are nothing will happen," the dragon said as she slid carefully alongside the man.

Smiling, she continued, "By the way, my name is Ekiya, and the loud one here is Pushan, and together we run Faraway Castle," she said with a polite bow. "I'd take you to your room, but the shift will happen at any moment, and it's probably better just to have a seat here instead of moving around when it happens."

As if on cue, a bright light engulfed the area shining through the windows and doors, followed by a strong pull to the ground. Pushan and Ekiya caught themselves managing to get in a squatting position while both Morrigan and Verthandi landed flat on their faces. They tried to get up but were unable to do little more than push their heads up off the ground. After a few minutes, the pull lessened, and the light faded.

"They couldn't make that any gentler?" Morrigan asked as she slowly got to her feet. Before anyone could answer they heard a loud roar.

"Well, that's not good," Ekiya quipped. She headed out the door with the others close behind her. Looking up they saw a large gathering of dragons in the sky. At the front was a large dragon that by itself seemed to blacken the sky with scales as black as night and two large wings that seemed to stretch for miles. Its large claws had a red hue to them, and it dwarfed most of the other dragons present.

"Ho-ly sin its Head Dragon Luna," Verthandi remarked as the dragon once again let out a loud roar. By now some of the other dragons had emerged from the buildings and were flying up to meet the hoard that was hovering above them.

Before they could even clear the height of the buildings, Luna opened its left upper claw, and a black ball began to form. It did the same with its right upper claw and merged the two balls together before firing it off at the ascending dragons. The ball quickly expanded as it left Luna's claws, making evading it impossible. It landed on the ground, leaving a large crater and a lot of dragon bodies.

"You dare to oppose our rules and laws? You would side with those who caused our kin much death and destruction? As did our ancestors before us, so too must you fall before your plague spreads to more of our kin."

"They sound like the Rannsoknardomari," Morrigan commented as the dragons gathered in the sky were screeching and roaring their approval of Luna' speech.

"They are one in the same; neither believes the other should be trusted. At least in close proximity."

"But I ask the same question, how does an organisation remain alive for so long if we've been truly separated for centuries!"

"I'd tell you to ask Luna, but he's not one who is good at listening. For now, though, I suggest you run. Our cover has been blown and Luna will burn this town to the ground. Go back into the inn and behind the counter is a trap door. That door will lead you to safety. Wait at least two days before trying to return here. Although I'm not sure how you will return your charge back to Terra."

"What about you guys?" Morrigan asked.

"We'll follow. What's a host that can't protect their guests?" Ekiya grinned.

"Ok," Morrigan nodded before her and Verthandi both disappeared back into the inn.

"You're a terrible liar," Pushan said as he approached Ekiya's side, closing the door.

"Am I?" she grinned to herself. "But so long as a seer lives, maybe, one day, we'll be able to have a life like this again. If not us, maybe our progeny. A world where we do not despise each other, but a world where we can live and laugh as one." Luna's maw then started to glow white, and a light seemed to ooze through his teeth as a grin seemed to spread across his face. Ekiya reached out and put her claw in Pushan's hand. "At least we'll be at the arches... together."

Pushan turned and embraced Ekiya, "We sure will, we sure will." Moments later Luna opened his maw, a bright white flame engulfed the town, sending out a shockwave as it hit. Even before the dust settled, the gathering hoard flew down and continued razing the town with their much smaller flames.

Chapter 13

Morrigan and Verthandi fought to maintain their footing as the ground shook violently in the underground escape cave. Soil and pebbles fell from the ceiling. Then there was a rumble in the distance.

"Uh-oh," Verthandi said as she looked behind them into the darkness. Before Morrigan could say anything Verthandi grabbed her, threw Morrigan over her shoulder and made an attempt at flying out as the pebbles falling from the ceiling started getting larger. Morrigan then became aware of the approaching rumble and saw in the distance the lights disappearing.

"It's collapsing!"

"Yes, I know, just hold still! Your squirming isn't making this any easier!" Verthandi ordered before moments later the cave-in overtook them. Verthandi wrapped her wings around both herself and Morrigan to protect them from the debris flow, but something still hit Morrigan on the head hard enough that she suffered a concussion and was knocked out.

When Morrigan's vision returned, it was in black and white, and she was sitting at the edge of a clearing in a heavily wooded area. There was a gathering of four dragons in a cross formation around a cloaked figure in the centre. One she recognized as Verthandi. The one to her left was a lighter hue than Verthandi, which she recognized as Sol. The one across from Verthandi appeared to be Luna. Another dragon sitting to the right of Verthandi was a darker hue, but she could not be completely certain of the dragon's identity, but maybe it was the one responsible for the fallout with Katherine's Village she had seen in the flashback.

"You hold too much power! You are the daughter of a dragon *and* a Terrakonan! Your future is shrouded in so much haze that even we cannot determine it!" the lightest hue dragon yelled.

"Tis true," Luna responded with a growl. "You would not be a mere Terrakonan, but something new, a fae. I must say though, Kronos, you have really outdone yourself on this one," Luna said as he looked to his right.

"Indeed, it took a lot to stabilise her enough to accept dragon essence," Kronos lauded. "However, just as you said, she has now surpassed the abilities of any current Terrakonan and even some of the younger wyrmlings."

"Don't I get a say in this?" Verthandi interrupted. "She's my Terrakonan and we really enjoy each other's company."

"Company or not, she is far too powerful for one sentient!" Luna yelled. He then pointed towards Kronos, "Kronos, destroy all your remaining faes and leave no trace that such a thing existed!"

"But what about—"

"Do it or be banished from Tumahab!" Luna thundered.

Kronos nodded meekly and then turned to fly off, barely hovering above ground, head hanging low. Luna then approached the cloaked figure and removed their hood. They looked up from the ground and smiled weakly, but Morrigan gasped. Looking at Verthandi was her own reflection.

"It's ok Morrigan. If this is what it takes to keep the peace, then I'm willing to go through with it," Morrigan's former self said. "It might be a lifetime before we find each other again, but I promise you I won't leave you immortal and alone. We'll meet again." Tears began forming and streaking down Verthandi's face as she moved forward.

"No, don't do it!" Morrigan got up and tried to run towards Verthandi. "No! Don't do it!" her vision faded. When she blinked, she was on the ground again looking upwards into Verthandi's face.

"Welcome back," Verthandi said.

"I..." Morrigan tried to say something, but nothing came out. Instead, she threw herself at Verthandi and hugged her tightly. "I'm back," she sobbed.

"What's wrong, you were screaming and fighting all that time, now you came out and you're crying?" Verthandi said, wrapping her wings around Morrigan.

"I... saw... in the past... Luna... ordered you to kill me," she sniffled.

Verthandi froze at the remark for a brief moment before sighing and lowering her head, "Yes... I did. I didn't know what else to do." She paused a moment before trying to look again towards Morrigan, "You were a new Terrakonan and we had already begun bonding. But then Kronos learned that you were a highly capable sentient not only in a physical capacity, but mentally as well. You also possessed superior healing skills and control. After the Vision of Destruction, Luna felt you were the cause of such destruction and ordered you killed. I wanted to refuse, but the vision plagued us and there was no denying it would happen unless we acted." She hung her head crying, "I'm sorry, I didn't mean for it to come to you like this. Ever since we first met, I thought about telling you everything. *Everything*. But the chance never materialised." Verthandi sniffled as she lowered her head and continued speaking quieter as her voice began to quiver. "She died over one thousand years ago, how could you be her? I pushed you, trying to get you at the same level as she was. Searching that maybe something would jolt your memory and you'd come back to me. But with every failure, I doubted you were really her. I doubted we could ever be friends like she was, so I never told you."

Morrigan reached up, touching Verthandi's face in an attempt to wipe away her tears. But since Verthandi's tears were bigger than Morrigan's hand, as she went to wipe away the tears, the water streamed down Morrigan's arm, dousing her with water. "Then I guess we're both failures," she said with a weak smile. "But from now on, let's work together and be winners. Fix our past failures. Okay?"

Verthandi rested her claw on Morrigan's hand and closed her eyes. "Sure," she said quietly nuzzling Morrigan.

"I guess, I should also apologise for yelling at you back at the Rannsoknardomari stronghold. When I blamed you for being selfish in keeping me alive."

Verthandi put a digit up to Morrigan's mouth and shook her head. "You didn't know. The fault was mine for not saying anything even then." She opened her eyes, "But there is one thing you must know before moving on."

"O-okay?" Morrigan responded.

Verthandi brought Morrigan's hand down from her face, placing both palms face up between both her claws. She then took in a deep breath and let out a long exhale before speaking. "Remember Minda?"

Morrigan slowly nodded, "The old hermit lady?"

"Yes, her. Well, she's your mother. I suspect the reason she sent you away so quickly was because she didn't want anything to remind her of…" there was a small pause, Verthandi looked at Morrigan dead in the eyes before continuing, "Kronos."

"I don't get it," Morrigan shrugged.

"Kronos and Minda are your parents." Verthandi looked off outside the cave as she continued, "After the Vision of Destruction, Kronos took it upon himself to try to find someone who would be able to see an alternate future. None of the Seer Dragons would support his work, so he worked on his own daughter to enhance the ability. This would have driven a wedge between the two normally, but Kronos buried himself in his work." She then refocused her gaze back in front of her, "Minda… felt alone and isolated, even from her own child. She called out to him, but there was never any response. And so one day she severed her link to Kronos. He didn't even feel it; he was so devoted to his work. He only noticed some time later that she was not there."

Verthandi sighed heavily and hung her head, "That combined with the loss of you in particular broke him. He went on a rampage, a rampage that those who went on to establish the Rannsoknardomari remember dragons as. Large, out of control brutes that rained destruction on all they touch." She looked back towards Morrigan, a forlorn expression on her face. "Even after he regained some semblance of sanity, he remained a broken dragon as he had lost his mate, his progeny and his work were rendered useless. He then struck out at Minda's family, but that only angered the sentients more." She paused again, a heavy sigh escaping her lips during the brief interlude between sentences. "This prompted the sentients to strike back, starting what the sentients called the Terrakonan War. The dragons called them the Wild War as the war borne from Kronos' wild chase looking for Minda. In an attempt to perform a clean cut and end the way, Minda created a rift. The rift allowed her to return to Terra and when she closed the gate, she knew she would safely be away from Kronos and that his rampage would end with her out of his reach, effectively dead to him."

"And she never looked back?" Morrigan asked.

Verthandi sighed, "She did. She never outright said it, but in conversations with Terrakonans over the years, she admits to missing him. However, she vowed never to reopen the Asterian Gate again. Kronos has tried to open the gate but has never been successful. Luna had him put to sleep to prevent further deterioration, and Luna of course, doesn't want the sentients to mix back with us so he had that as an extra incentive."

"Why not just kill him?" Morrigan asked.

"Because he is effectively immortal. Even though Minda had severed her link with Kronos, the essence still existed between them. More so as they had you. Thus, unless they killed Minda he could seep essence from her and just resurrect himself. And as he no longer has his soulmate with him, he doesn't age. Ever forward until we find ourselves together under the timeless arch," she added with a sigh.

"What if someone killed Minda or she died of old age?"

She can't die of old age either. Her soul is bound to Kronos. As for trying to kill her, remember she still maintains her Terrakonan powers. If they did locate her, they'd have to admit to killing someone who, if you believe everything out of the council… helped make Tumahab a better place for dragons to live. Additionally, only the four you saw in your flashback are aware of this circumstance. That being Kronos, Luna, me and the other one that was killed after they tried to rebel against the council named Sol."

"So why not reunite them? Even if it's in Ardivian Space?" Morrigan asked. "It can't be that hard to reawaken Kronos, can it?"

"No, but convincing Luna that anything good would come of it is the hard part."

"Can't we just avoid him completely?"

Verthandi frowned and then laughed. "No, Luna is not simply one you can simply avoid. He watches his territory very, *very* closely. For instance, if a rock drops, he's there to investigate. And if he doesn't come, his minions will."

"And you're saying there is no way around this?"

Chapter 14

Verthandi looked at Morrigan, closed her eyes and grinned to herself. "Of course. Nogomain can offer you a way in with some sort of spirit blending."

"So let's go!" Morrigan jumped up.

"In a world where a sentient has not been seen in *aeons*, transporting you around is not exactly easy," Verthandi said as she tried to get Morrigan to sit back down again. "If any should see you it would be immediately questioned."

"But how did you get me from the cave to here? It couldn't have been *that* convenient of a tunnel," Morrigan frowned.

"We're in a cave possibly in the Hinterlands as I haven't sensed many dragons going by." She then looked out towards the cave entrance, "But I at least will have to leave soon, as my absence would be noted, especially by Luna if I failed to show up at the council."

"Oh…" Morrigan said as she plopped back down on the ground. There were a few moments of silence before Morrigan's face lit back up again. "How do you usually carry things? You'd need a way to transport food and water. Katherine said you guys have shops and merchants, and if that's true it also means there has to be some means of carrying your goods around."

"Well yes, there are sacs, but I don't have any on me," Verthandi shrugged. "I guess I can go home and get one and carry you back with some other goods. You'd probably be really tightly packed, unless I brought some lighter items."

"Just don't bring anything like rocks or wood that would crush me or anything alive that would have me kicking and screaming all the way." Both laughed at the comment.

"No, I promise it won't be any of those," Verthandi responded as she regained her composure. She then turned to head out of the cave entrance. "Just sit tight. Hopefully this isn't too far into the Hinterlands so I should be back within a few hours."

"I will," Morrigan nodded.

With that Verthandi spread her wings and flew off, while Morrigan sat back down at the back of the cave. She wasn't seated for long before she started curling her hair around her fingers thinking about being in Tumahab.

All of a sudden, a thought occurred to her, and she stopped curling her hair. If Verthandi thought she was Minda's daughter, Minda obviously would have thought the same. Yet Minda seemed almost in a rush to get rid of her. Why?

Getting up from her seat she paced to the entrance and looked out. "Is there something else I'm missing?" she thought aloud. "Well duh, I don't remember even living for that long," she said, bopping her head with her hand.

Then she paced back to where she had been sitting, "But if I'm really that old, could I be suffering from the same amnesia as Charlie and Gilbert?" As she stared at the wall, she noticed a line, followed by dots. Moving closer towards the wall she followed the lines and dots that eventually disappeared.

She brushed away the area and found that more of them were hidden along the wall. Rolling her left sleeve up past her hands she used it to help her dust off the message. The dots and dashes ran the length of the wall and were three rows deep. She ran her hands over the message, "Morse? I didn't think anyone physically wrote this," she mused. She closed her eyes and started from the top feeling for spacing between the letters and words, making an internal beep as she went through the message. Once she thought she had it figured out, she began reciting the message as she ran her hand along it.

To the finder of this message, I apologise for using ancient script, but it is the only way to communicate without fear of persecution from our pursuers. Beware of Sol and Luna. Together they shall eclipse the world of reason and mould it to their own.

Even with the gap, they shall not be deterred. They turned our parents against each other and they slayed our sister. We continue to search for a solution, but Luna has consolidated his power and shadows our every move. We are heading to Asteria to hopefully find a solution and safety. May the fates ever be kind to us, and to whomever reads this may the wings of strength and patience guide you towards a brighter future than ours. Regards, Ardivia Fae.

She slowly opened her eyes back up as she reached the end of the message. She remained there sitting for a while, feeling a weight in her stomach. "Beware Luna and Sol," she said with a blank stare. "Luna… I've seen. But Sol is dead." She then ran her fingers back over the message, "But it's obvious the divide has been established, yet the writer still insists that they will still overcome even that." As her thoughts raced around this fact, she felt a sharp pain in her head. She closed her eyes, wincing as she dropped down on all fours.

She saw an image of two people in a dark space. One person was Minda, the other she didn't know, but they had large feathery wings, similar to what Katherine and Nome looked like when they were preparing to take flight.

"Please, Mother Minda take this," the winged one spoke as they shoved something into Minda's hand. "I know you have forsaken the dragons and probably to a degree us Fae but keep this for when our sister returns."

"She's dead, what good will this do other than bring me grief?" Minda scowled as she held the winged person's hand from leaving hers.

"She's not dead! She yet lives! Nogomain has assured me that her spirit is not yet broken, but simply drifts, healing so that one day it may return to us. Please take it. It's unlikely we'll find her before you. You're her mother; she'll come back to you first."

"Why not come through the gate with us? The humans have no need for your essence, and you can escape the ravages of war."

The winged one shook their head, "No. That is not my lot. We will continue on this side in case she returns unto us, but it is unlikely." He then rammed his shoulder into her and pushed her through a shimmering pool that had been behind her. "Goodbye Mother. Please take care of our sister, and I'll watch over Father," the winged person said as the shimmering faded, and the roar of dragons could be heard approaching.

The winged person turned to walk out as the image faded away from her. She tried to refocus as the person turned slightly. Though Morrigan felt the person was directly looking at her, all she could see was a smug grin, but no distinguishable features. Her pain lessened as the focus and image fully faded. She slowly opened her eyes as the last bit of pain went away, finding herself back in the cave. A few moments later, she became aware of a winged beast near the entrance to the cave.

Chapter 15

"I'm back!" Verthandi announced.

As she came farther into the cave, she began to panic at the site of Morrigan's condition. Morrigan barely stood, rubbing her head with her eyes partially opened and gritting her teeth. She quickly added, "What happened to you? Run yourself into a rock?"

"No," Morrigan said as she stopped rubbing her temple. "There was a hidden message here from Ardivia Fae warning us to be careful of Luna and Sol."

"Sol is dead though," Verthandi responded. "So both aren't really a threat, and where did you come across this message? It could simply be a case of slander or Rannsoknardomari propaganda."

"No, look, it's written right here," Morrigan said as she motioned towards the wall behind her. Verthandi approached the wall and squinted her eyes to look at it.

"It's a bunch of dots and dashes. How are you so sure it's a real message?"

"We normally use it as a series of flickers. A dot is one short flash, and a line has the light exposed for three times the length as the dot." Verthandi had a sceptical look on her face as Morrigan added, "In the opening line, the writer says they use this method because the dragons would not understand it. I guess even with close relations, there were still some things they kept away from you." She turned, looking at the message and recited it for Verthandi.

Verthandi's eyes widened, mouth agape as Morrigan mentioned the writer's name. Looking away she lowered her head, "So Ardivia survived and headed to Asteria huh?"

"What's wrong?" Morrigan asked, crossing her arms. "Still don't believe me?"

"Oh, no, nothing of the sort," Verthandi snapped up her head refocusing back on Morrigan without maintaining eye contact, "Ardivia was your little brother. When Kronos went on his rampage, the one they used to quell him was Ardivia. He had agreed to help in exchange the Fae would be respected members of society. It never happened. Instead, the Fae were killed off, just as the sentients before them." She paused briefly. "Oh… No," she exclaimed, snapping her neck up stiffly.

"Oh no what?" Morrigan asked.

"Your vision, the one with the crystals," Verthandi stammered shivering.

"What about it?"

"The crystals are anchor crystals. If I remember correctly, Kronos had discovered a method to extract Fae's essence and crystalized it. A sentient that comes into contact with it harbours actual dragon essence instead of just the residual amount from bonding. They become a literal capture jar for whatever dragon they are bonded to."

"I don't get it," Morrigan shrugged. "Human and dragon are already bonded. What difference does it make?"

If you trigger the reaction, the dragon's essence would be trapped on the other side of the divide. Their body would be soulless and easily manipulated. You would create an instant blind loyal army."

"But what of the essence and soul on the other side?"

"No sentient is meant to take that much strain. Think about Katherine, after her rage, she was obviously not well enough to even join her sister at the library. This is even after you recall Nome was close enough to death that Katherine lost it when you last saw her."

"But how would you transfer these crystals across the divide?"

"Via another Terrakonans or... a dragon."

"But we've had this conversation before, there are no dragons on the other"

"No! There is! The one that destroyed your village, the one that killed my previous Terrakonans. The dragon is the true form. It is not a manifestation, it's the actual form. Oh, how could I have been so *stupid*!" she wailed falling flat on the ground, thumping her claws as she hit the ground.

"Stupid about what?"

"*Everything!* Luna and Sol have been playing us for fools since he came back and announced he had killed Sol." She remained on all fours and Morrigan rubbed her side.

"We've all been fooled once or twice. But is there a way to reverse it?"

Verthandi growled her answer, "We fly to Nogomain, and make him answer to us."

"Nogomain? Not Asteria?"

"Yes, Nogomain," Verthandi growled. "I should have confronted him centuries ago about the massacres, but I looked the other way. He had the council's blessing, and it would have simply looked as an old seer was trying to recapture the glory back away from the council."

"Okay, Nogomain it is," Morrigan said, taking a few steps away.

"It's not your fault," Verthandi growled, rising back up on her hind legs. "This anger is not directed at you, but to others. Especially after spending time belittling me, making me feel like I was the failure." She opened her sac, "Get in and wrap yourself well, the trip shouldn't be long, but if you want to make sure you stay warm, wrap up."

Morrigan looked inside and saw the sac was about half filled with moss mats. She climbed in, wrapping herself in the mats before telling Verthandi she was ready. Verthandi cradled the sac in her forearms before spreading her wings and taking off Northward.

The trip itself wasn't very long, or at least it wasn't to Morrigan. She had nestled herself into the moss and despite hearing the sac flap in the wind, she never felt a hint of cold air. The smell of the moss had a soothing effect on her, and she felt compelled to rest her eyes, if just for a moment letting out a contented sigh. The next thing she knew, she was disturbed by a jarring thud as Verthandi landed back on the ground.

"We're here," Verthandi said, lowering the sac to the ground. Morrigan was greeted by a dark and hazy landscape as she crawled out of the sac. She felt a little chill and shivered as she got out and on the ground. There was no smell of sorts, nor was there anything that appeared to be of the living in the immediate vicinity.

"Why is it so cold here? I don't see any snow nor is it windy?"

"It's the spirits," Verthandi responded as she put the sac over her shoulder. "Nogomain gathers them, and they help him communicate with the great beyond. When wandering or dead spirits touch the living, they cause a cold feeling. It's where the notion of a cold person has a cold spirit comes from. Nogomain should be a little up ahead, I'm sure he heard us landing." She then placed one of her claws next to Morrigan, "Hop on; just so that no one steps on you, or he get any ideas and you stray too far."

Morrigan climbed into Verthandi's claw which she partially closed around her. Verthandi then walked around a sharp bend and into a cavern. There, sitting on a pile of what looked like urns was Nogomain.

"I figured it was you," he growled as Verthandi approached. "Angered and enraged."

"Cut it out!" Verthandi interrupted Nogomain. "I want to know what happened with the Fae Massacre and Soul Crystals!"

Nogomain paused and growled, "Why reopen healed wounds. Doing so will only bring back the pain and suffering long since passed."

"We want the truth!" Verthandi snapped.

"We?" Nogomain asked before noticing Morrigan in Verthandi's claw. "So you not only seek to bring up old wounds, but also actively break the rules of society by bringing her here. Did you not learn anything from your past? We will simply be forced to kill them again."

"No, you will only kill to satisfy your own!" Morrigan fired off. "The Rannsoknardomari and the council are one in the same. What's wrong with us living together? Even when presented with a successful example, Luna burned it to ashes, while the Rannsoknardomari are so zealous in their purge they aren't even willing to listen to reason. Why? How do both of you have a lead group that is so fervent in their belief that peace cannot be attained by working together?"

"Silence little one!" Nogomain thundered. "You are talking about things you know nothing about. Even your beloved partner here took part in the massacre, going so far as to kill you herself in cold blood." Nogomain then turned his back to them, "I have at least tried to atone for those sins. Caring for Katherine and seeing her love and care for others has helped me heal from those dark times."

"Live with or forget?" Verthandi seethed. "You have become so self-catered in your belief that you are helping those you once harmed, you have turned a blind eye to what got you there in the first place."

"Silence!" he bellowed, whirling around to face them. "I know I did wrong. We wiped out the Fae because they reminded us of the sentients. Was it right at the time? Absolutely! Many of them had spirits of rage and would have turned on us given the chance, just as their ancestors did."

His posture opened, as he fell to the ground, "We could only answer blood with more blood. We were no better, but for so long we held that we were, and it was a heavy burden on my conscience." He looked up at Morrigan, "But then Katherine became my Terrakonan. I met her one night after her town had been attacked. My former Terrakonan was caught in the attack and was badly injured. I was sure I'd lose my Terrakonan that day, but then she appeared and attempted to help him get out." He paused looking at the ground before continuing, "'Why do you help others before helping yourself? Why not escape and leave me behind?' I asked her. She did not answer, but I could feel her legs shaking, her breathing was heavy in between coughs. She cared not for her own safety or well-being as the fire roared all around them. At that point I realised that that was the person I wanted to be.

"She plopped us down on the ground at the forest edge. 'Why?' I asked one more time. 'Why not?' she responded back with a weak smile. My former Terrakonan knew they would not survive the night. With what remaining energy they had, they infused Katherine, and she became my Terrakonan. That was the first time I ever saw tears for anything but sadness. As she explained it to me, I found there was much I had to learn. She taught me of care and empathy. I taught her about our history and logic. She showed me to look ahead and not live in the past. That we all make mistakes; that we should learn from them, and not to be afraid to make them in the first place."

"And what of the crystals? Did you forget about those too? All the posturing you do, to justify your 'new' self?" Verthandi fired. "You're so afraid of making the same mistake twice that you pretend everything else never happened. You abandoned us once and now again in an effort to put yourself on higher ground than the rest of us."

"What about the crystals?" Nogomain asked. "I righted that wrong. Yes, we gained them from the Fae Massacre, but we destroyed them as per Luna' orders."

"Did you?" Morrigan asked.

"She has the gift Nogomain," Verthandi said as Nogomain was about to retort. Nogomain's mouth hung open upon hearing this.

"But no one has seen a vision for over one thousand years."

"I know, I'm one of the old seers, yet she has the ability which we've lacked. Why that is, I do not know, but what I do know is her visions are what brought us here."

"Oh, I can help you with that," a voice came from the cave entrance. They turned around and saw a white dragon blocking the entrance. It was on all fours, wings tucked neatly on its back like a bird, a sly grin dancing across its face.

Chapter 16

"Oh my, consorting with a sentient," the dragon gasped as it spied Morrigan. "You two have really done it now."

"Thomas, you being here can never be a good sign," Nogomain seethed as he got back to his feet.

"I'm *so* hurt you'd think that," Thomas remarked sarcastically putting his fore claw to its head. He then put his claw down flashing a toothy smile. "She retains the ability because she has avoided the suppressants. Long before any of us were around, there was an oath taken that in exchange for divining powers, no dragon blood was to ever be consumed. The war brought along with it dragon blood from both dragons and fae. Whether intentional or unintentional, dragon blood was consumed by dragon, fae and sentient alike. All except for her as she was killed before the war happened. How she escaped all this time is beyond me, but I'll happily return her to the pit she emerged from."

He then sprang forward, lunging straight towards Morrigan. Verthandi barely moved her hand out of Thomas' pathway, feeling his teeth graze on the outside of her claw. As he landed and turned to make a second lunge, Nogomain grabbed him by the wings attempting to grapple him to the ground.

"Release me Nogomain!" Thomas hissed. "The council will not stand for this! You know what they would do if they found a sentient here! You know what would happen should you assist them and not me!" Thomas then let out a loud screech as Nogomain sank his claws into him. Thomas tried to buffet Nogomain with his wings, but Nogomain caught them in his mouth yanking them away from his back, causing Thomas to arch and screech again in pain. When Nogomain released Thomas's wings, they fell ruffled and limp to the side.

"I am well aware of what the consequences are. However, I have turned a blind eye long enough to your master. These two are right; I have forgotten who I was in the past. I have forgotten what it's like to stand and fight. For too long I have run away, but today I will not run or hide any longer." Nogomain roared and spread his own wings. His figure seemed to lose its shape and become almost ethereal; a growing dark plume filled the cave. "Go to Taben's Pyre, there you will find the answers you seek. For this time, do not look back."

"But we can—" Verthandi started to say before Nogomain let out another roar that shook the cave and ground, scattering his pile of urns. Verthandi flinched back and nodded before quickly turning tail and leaving.

"Good," Nogomain growled. He then returned his attention back, flipping Thomas over on his back before leaning down and touching him, snout to snout.

As they touched, the ethereal look hardened to reveal a black dragon with a much larger wingspan. The wings were large enough that they had their own set of claws. Nogomain was on all fours and had an elongated neck and his incisors stuck out of his jaw. "Hello old friend," Nogomain's voice sounded a great deal younger and deeper.

"No... Nashmaw we killed you," Thomas gasped as he tried to wiggle free from beneath Nogomain's girth.

"You did, and I applaud you for it," Nogomain spoke, raising his head in the air.

"Then... how...?" Thomas stammered.

"Your crystal jar seals, but every jar has a lid. Together me and Katherine opened that lid. I do say it was quite the extravagant ploy, giving her a crystal and then sending her to me, believing that I'd never find out. But she was a very curious individual, and her curiosity drove her to seek answers I'd never have found on my own. We found a way to flip your plan and seal away just enough that Nashmaw doesn't surface." He then sneered as he brought his wing claws down to each side of Thomas's head. "You should have realised what was going on when she thrashed your Terrakonan. But worry not poor Thomas; your fate will be a lot faster and merciful than your Terrakonan's. However, it will have the same resolution, a dark end in my maw."

In one fell swoop Nogomain severed Thomas's head from his body, staining the formerly white body of Thomas bright red. As the blood began to flow along the floor it turned to dark red and then black. The urns, originally an earthy brown colour, began shifting their shade to black as they came into contact with the blood.

"Drink well my spirits. Not since before the Great Divide have you drunk so deeply," Nogomain laughed as he and his entire cave turned black. Leaving only a haunting echo and two glowing blood red eyes.

....

Verthandi flew quickly towards Taben's Pyre. She didn't get Morrigan fully into the sac, her head stuck out of the opening. Morrigan had pulled some of the moss and the edges of the sac up to her face to try to keep warm. She felt a popping sensation in her ear just before a bolt of lightning flashed right in front of Verthandi. Stopping short, Verthandi clamped her claw hard on Morrigan.

"A little softer next time," Morrigan wheezed.

"Sorry, but I didn't want you to go tumbling." Verthandi looked up and saw a dragon descending to them. As she prepared to move off, another wall of lightning flash and blocked her path. "Arnhem, I don't have time for your antics," Verthandi growled as Arnhem reached her eye level.

"Neither do I intend to take up much of your time, but a word of caution."

"Do you even know what that word means?" Verthandi remarked with an eye roll.

"Luna is gathering at Taben's Pyre. If you do intend to continue on, be very careful, especially with your Terrakonan."

"We have to face Luna sooner or later, unless you have an alternate course of action, we are still headed to the pyre."

"You will not be able to defend yourself and your Terrakonan," Arnhem rumbled. "Luna has started gathering his army at the pyre. What it is he seeks appears to be the gate. Yet why something so simple seems… beneath Luna."

"Your speculation is not very helpful," Verthandi frowned. "While your warning is timely, it doesn't help with moving forward." She flapped her wings rapidly ascending above Arnhem flying past him.

"Shouldn't we have perhaps listened to him?" Morrigan asked.

"If he had a more constructive route, yes. But it would be better to go to the source and get first-hand information rather than speculate." She then let the bottom of the sac slip out of her hand, causing Morrigan to fall further inside the sac. "Wrap up, at the very least if Luna really is at the pyre, we can't have him or any of his friends spying you." Morrigan did not respond as she tried to make herself comfortable. Verthandi gave her a few minutes before pulling the sac back up and cradling it in her arms. Soon a large rock tower formation came into view, its black rock glistening in the rays of the setting sun. At its base was a gathering of dragons and at the front Verthandi spied the large figure of Luna.

"Verthandi, glad you could make it," Luna said as Verthandi landed. "I didn't know if you would make it. After missing the last council meeting there were rumours circulating that you were aiding a hidden city where sentients and dragons were living together."

"I assure you; I'd do nothing of the sort," Verthandi responded. "I was simply not well, so I went out to gather some draknip," she said as she lowered her sac. Luna was offered a quick look in before Verthandi closed the sac back up.

"Very well," Luna responded.

"By the way, what's with this city you speak of? Is that why you've gathered everyone?" Verthandi asked with a nervous laugh. She was twiddling with the edge of the sac before throwing it over on her back.

"What was that?" Luna snapped up as he thought he heard a yelp.

Chapter 17

"What was what?" Verthandi grinned as she shifted her weight around.

"It almost sounded like a sentient scream," he growled as he looked around, craning his neck to see if he could hear the sound again or see a sentient scurrying about hiding.

"Oh, come now," Verthandi said as she pats him on the back with her free arm, "Sentients haven't been seen here for *aeons*, not to mention if one *did* happen to get through, I'm sure they'd be immediately hunted and killed. Or maybe it's just your anticipation of destroying As… city."

Luna laughed and raised his fists, "We already destroyed the pest. I have learned that it is best to act sooner rather than later. Never give them the chance to escape otherwise they will have time to poison others."

"Then why are we gathering here?"

"Today we open the gate," Luna grinned. Clenching his claw in his fist he seethed, "Today we take vengeance on the sentients for all the trouble they have brought us."

"We could have just gathered and left from the Council Seats," Verthandi frowned. "Why gather at the pyre?"

"Kronos has been *dying* to get to the gate," he chuckled. "What better way than to let him go to the gate and open it for us." At that moment a pillar of light shot off into the sky. "And that would be our cue," Luna grinned, letting out a loud roar, and the others gathered following suit.

Looking back at Verthandi, Luna said, "Stay here if you need to recover your strength. I don't imagine we'd have much of a fight on the other side." Then he turned, gathering the hoard, "To wing my brothers and sisters! Let the last thing they hear be our Battle Wing Song!" He yelled, taking off. The others took off behind him in V-shaped formations behind him singing:

From the sky above, gazing down on the world.

To see the endless taint of the sentient.

Black with hatred and conquest their blackened souls threaten.

Come fight O brave ones! Claws, teeth and scales cast in glorious flight.

Their lives are remembered in valiant songs.

And like rivers their blood shall run.

Running down our claws. Running down our bodies. Flow until our vengeance has been sated.

And then we will fly in a world born anew. Glorious and free of their taint.

Until then, the war shall rage on! The bold will fight on.

Until there is nothing left of their existence but an echo of song.

Verthandi did not join in the chorus but flew with one of the peripheral V-formations. She felt a little sick to her stomach as the dragons beat their wings in time with the tune, remaining in perfect sync as they flew.

As they drew closer to the pillar of light a large shadow loomed in front of them. As if forming from inside the haze, two blood red eyes peered through seemingly emitting a low growl and wings spread across the sky like a blanket blotting out everything in front of them as they extended out from the main body. Luna and the others were forced to stop as the dragon let out a thunderous roar that ripped through the air enough to create turbulence.

"Do not obstruct us Nogomain!" Luna yelled before adding with a growl, "Or should I say, Divine Dragon Nashmaw."

With that revelation the haze seemed to fade, revealing a large black dragon on all fours with two pairs of wings on its back, stretched out to their maximum span. "You will not pass this point Luna," Nashmaw spoke with a voice that resonated and echoed within everyone. "Your days of trickery and deception are over."

Verthandi started to shiver as a black haze seemed to ooze from the ground rising towards the gathered dragons. Some of the other dragons began backing off, putting distance between themselves and Luna.

"Nashmaw, you may have been mighty in the past, but you have become old and soft. I will not allow you to hinder our progress!" Luna yelled defiantly as he produced a black coloured crystal in his hand. "I didn't want to play this so soon, but you leave me no choice," Luna said with a sly grin.

The crystal flashed black and slowly as if water were being poured into it, changed to a clear crystal. Verthandi and Morrigan bent forward as if someone punched them in the stomach. There was a short pain in their heads, but it soon passed. The flash however, had no visible effect on Nashmaw. All that anyone could see was a white coloured ripple emanating from the base of his neck, spreading out like shockwaves across the open sky. The other dragons seemed to show little bother with the flash.

"Your trickery will not work on me," Nashmaw sneered.

"No, not you, but the others it works on," Luna said triumphantly as the other dragons gathered let out a combined ear-splitting screech. They then broke their formations and charged towards Nashmaw.

"Your soulless dolls are still of no concern to me," Nashmaw stated as he swept his wings back before executing a mighty flap, causing a great gale to occur in front of him. Luna climbed higher in the sky in order to avoid getting swept away, while Verthandi flew further to the side. The hoard of dragons became a tangled mess as they fought to remain airborne in the face of unfamiliar wind currents. A few managed to fly through the turbulence and maintain their attacking flight path. Right at the last minute, before they struck him, Nashmaw adjusted his wings to generate enough lift to vertically raise himself off the ground, before crashing back to the ground, trampling the attackers underfoot.

"Verthandi help them!" Luna ordered as Nashmaw lashed out at him.

"I suggest you leave here," Nashmaw growled before unleashing a black flame that merged with the strong gale from the flap to form a black tornado, which served to capture Luna within the vortex.

"Go," Verthandi heard Nogomain echo in her head. "I will hold them here. Until I am overwhelmed with numbers."

"Are you sure we can't assist?"

"Escape and you will be assisting."

"Alright," Verthandi nodded, turning, flying by Nashmaw's left wing tip.

By this time, Luna had finally fought free of the fire tornado. When it cleared a new hoard gathered. The dragons that had fallen to the ground were covered by the black haze on the ground. "I did not intend to fight you, but if it's a fight you want, it's a fight you'll get. Tumahab bows to me and soon you will too. We removed you once before and we shall remove you again!" Luna roared, signalling the newly assembled hoard to charge. This hoard was much larger than the original hoard that had attacked Nashmaw earlier.

The black haze leapt from the ground engulfing the entire area, turning it pitch black. "In the darkness, you will find the comfort of death's cold embrace," Nashmaw said before closing his eyes. When he opened them, he was on the seaside; the sun was slowly setting beyond the horizon, adding a red tint to both the sky and the waves. Katherine was standing ankle deep in the water looking out towards the horizon. He hugged her from behind and she put her hands over his.

"Long has been our journey, from the dark of night, almost to the twilight of the same. As the sun sets on us one last time, I just want to say thanks for everything. For putting up with an old cantankerous dragon."

Katherine laughed a little, closed her eyes, and leaned back into Nogomain. "I can say the same for you having to deal with a young, naïve human." A smile played on her lips as a single tear ran down her face, off her chin and onto Nashmaw's claw that was around her. Her voice quivered a little with a slight break, "but it was a wonderful journey." There was a small pause as a colourful arc formed around the sun. "So, what do you think is on the other side of the rainbow?"

"I don't know. You were the one that used to explain it to our daughter," Nogomain grinned.

"And now I understand why she never went to you for questions," Katherine sniffled. By now the arc had expanded to the point where it stopped growing and loomed directly in front of them. "Well whatever waits for us, beyond the arches, at least I have my favourite dragon for company," she added as she squeezed Nogomain's claws.

"Indeed, it shall," Nogomain said, hugging her tighter as the arc swallowed them.

"Take care, our daughter," Katherine whispered looking to the heavens, "May your guidance and judgement be as sharp and true as your lightning." Her eyes were saturated with tears, her voice now fully cracked and sniffling, "And don't ever forget where you came from, but always look forward to where you are going." Though her voice was no longer composed, she managed a bright smile, "Goodbye, world's best daughter, Nome. You certainly made life an adventure."

With that, she and Nogomain disappeared underneath the arc leaving behind nothing except the gentle sound of waves crashing along a sandy beach and a grey crystal, lodged in the sand where they had been standing. An image of Katherine and Nogomain briefly flashed on the top surface before the waves washed it away.

....

By now Verthandi had rushed towards the pillar of light descending rapidly to its base. There she found Kronos holding two crystals wedged in what appeared to be a flat stone. His focus was on his left claw, jaw closed tight, gritting his teeth as he tried to push it forward.

"Kronos! Stop!" Verthandi yelled as she landed, "Luna is using you!" she shrieked, dropping the bag rushing over to his side.

"I don't care!" he thundered without taking his eyes off the crystals. "All I want to do is see my beloved. I lost her once; I don't want to miss this chance to apologise to her."

"But you're going to bring the end of us!" Verthandi said as she grabbed the two crystals over Kronos' claws.

Kronos glared at Verthandi and pushed her off. "Away with you! You don't understand the hurt, the pain, the *suffering* I have been through. Even my sleep was haunted by the abandonment of my wife and my very own chil—
"

He stopped his rant as he spied Morrigan emerging from the sac. "You… came back here?" he said in a daze. "Am I so far gone that I'm hallucinating even while awake?" His grip loosened on the crystals and the white light began to wane.

Verthandi seized the moment to wrestle Kronos away from the controls to the ground. Tears began rolling down his eyes as he tried to reach out to Morrigan. "My daughter, only in dreams did I imagine I'd see you again. Come here my child."

Morrigan hesitated to move. "Ever cautious, just like your mother," Kronos smiled weakly, beckoning Morrigan to move closer to him. "It pains me that I can't even excuse why you don't know me." Verthandi slowly released him, allowing him to sit up on his two hind legs.

Morrigan looked towards Verthandi. She nodded towards her. Looking back at Kronos, Morrigan slowly walked towards him with her arms close to her slight leaning backwards. When she was close enough, he encircled her with his wings and carried Morrigan the last few metres. Kronos lifted Morrigan close to his snout. Morrigan tried to scramble away, but she could not find any traction on the wing. Tensing up she closed her eyes tightly raising her hands to guard herself from the grand beast.

However, instead of feeling aggression, she felt the gentle touch of Kronos' snout touching her hands. Indescribable warmth permeated her hands. It was not burning like a fire, but a settling, calming heat, like that of a campfire during a cool night. She moved her hands across his snout and as she leaned in and spread her embrace, she felt the warmness spread across her body, inviting her to continue the embrace. She let out a contented sigh.

"My dear daughter, I'm sorry you had to suffer so much in my absence," Kronos said as he shed a few tears. "You've grown so much since I last saw you, cradled in your mother's arms. Now you're big enough to cradle your own." He lowered himself to the ground and allowed Morrigan to climb off his snout onto the ground, "Can you ever forgive me for leaving you and your mother? Can you forgive the years of madness when I forsook you for what I thought was a higher calling?"

Morrigan looked him in the eye and walked over to Kronos. She put her hand on his face and wiped away his tears. "Dad, if that is what I call you, I forgive you. I'm sure you had your reasons, but being here with you, I feel... safe. I don't know why that is. I don't hold any malice toward you. I guess I can't miss what I've never had or have no memory of."

Kronos put a claw up to Morrigan's hand, "Thank you." He rose, turning towards Verthandi, "I won't take her from you this time, but are you able to recover her memory?"

Verthandi shook her head, "No. I've tried. I even doubted she was your daughter until a few moments ago."

"Then where have they gone?" Kronos cried.

Verthandi shrugged, paused and continued, "That is something we can worry about later. For now we need to destroy this gate before Noc—"

"No!" Kronos yelled. "I will make it through to the other side. My life will not be fulfilled until I apologise to Minda. If I feel hurt, I know she hurts more, and even though it has taken me aeons to realise, I will let her know I erred and I pray that she will forgive me." He paused his grip for a moment, though and lowered his voice slightly, "As it pains me my child is not safe here. The others would surely attempt to kill her, just as they attempted to kill her before. I will not again stand idly by while my family is torn to pieces!" He returned to the gate crystals with added vigour. "I will open the gate!" The white light returned back to its previous intensity.

"Might as well help him," Morrigan said to Verthandi. "He's set in his motivation."

"But!"

Morrigan shook her head, "I know how you feel, but he wants to do this. Now would be the best time while Nashmaw is holding up the invasion force. We could get a head start." Verthandi hesitated but Morrigan continued, "We both know how it feels to make mistakes, and we both know how the guilt eats at us. Look at him!" She motioned towards Kronos, "He's obviously a dragon on a mission. He wants to correct his mistakes, let's help him."

Verthandi looked over to Kronos. His jaw set in a grimace as he tried to force the controls to rotate. She looked back to Morrigan; her eyes still fixed on Kronos. "Ok, let's get this over with." Morrigan climbed into Verthandi's claw. Verthandi moved her claw from the ground to her shoulder, where Morrigan got off. Verthandi then walked towards Kronos and put her claws over his.

"Nothing you say will stop me!" he yelled.

"No, let's do this together," Morrigan replied.

Kronos was at a loss for words. He tried to move his mouth, but it didn't budge. He smiled weakly, "Thank you." They redoubled their efforts and soon the sky opened up to reveal another world. "That's it!" Kronos cried. A few moments later Morrigan felt herself floating upward before the pillar of light blinded her.

"Not who we expected through the gate," Morrigan heard a voice speak as her sight slowly came back into focus.

"Well, damn," Morrigan muttered as she was greeted by the same spectacle. Their backs were to a cliff but spread out in front of them was a sea of red and black.

Chapter 18

"Although I shouldn't be surprised that you'd find your way together." A woman moved forward and Morrigan recognized her as Solara.

"Wait! Don't kill these dragons!" Morrigan yelled as she moved between the crowd and the two dragons.

"Who said anything about slaying dragons?" she chuckled.

"But aren't you the…"

"Rannsoknardomari? Yes, we are. But killing either of these two was not part of the original idea." The smile then melted from her face and was replaced with a scowl. "In hindsight I should have killed you when we had the chance. However, I underestimated how far along you had come with Verthandi."

"Over my dead body!" Verthandi bellowed, unleashing green orbs into the gathered army. None made their mark as Solara blocked the attack. "What? How?"

"I admit Verthandi your powers have not waned since the last time I saw you, but you and your Terrakonan are a potential risk to our plan and must be dealt with." She raised her hand and in one unified sound everyone readied their weapons. "Just as you thought I would not see the New World

Order, so too will you now," she sneered, dropping her arm, unleashing a wave of arrows towards Kronos, Verthandi and Morrigan. Kronos extended his wings, forming a barrier around them. The arrows bounced harmlessly off the barrier to the ground.

"I should have figured you'd not go down so easily, but don't you worry, I've prepared a surprise for just such a case as this," Solara said, her voice growing deeper at the end of the sentence. A fire spread from her eyes that worked its way through her whole body, engulfing her and expanding until it took the form of a large gold dragon.

"Sol!" Kronos gasped.

"In the flesh," Sol responded. "Now to complete the task I started centuries ago and wipe out the last remnants of the seer dragons." She took in a deep breath, "and this time you won't have her to save you." When she exhaled, she breathed out a fire ball. It flexed the point on Kronos' barrier and forced him to reduce its size. He gathered his energy and forced back, exploding the barrier and dissipating the fire ball.

"So is that how it is," Kronos muttered. The pillar of light once again began to form and emerging from it was Luna and his dragon hoard.

"To wing!" Verthandi said. She grabbed Morrigan in her claw and began ascending. Kronos did the same, releasing a fireball to the ground to cover their ascent. Sol did not give chase but was instead content with blocking the attack, waiting for Luna's full emergence from the pillar of light. The last they heard was a joyous roar as Luna and his hoard made it through unscathed and unopposed.

"Come, we must find Minda at once!" Kronos said as he began to veer towards the West.

"Why? Your drive to see Minda you might as well say has cost us the inhabitants of Terra!" Verthandi fired back.

"They were coming through regardless," Kronos responded. "Whether it was today or a millennium from now. They already had the means, and as a former seer, Luna had all the tools they needed. They just needed a proper scapegoat, and I happily obliged."

"So, what happens if Minda rejects you?" Morrigan asked, sticking her head out from between Verthandi's claws.

"It doesn't matter. I will at the very least feel… released… from this burden." There was a small pause before he continued, "Even if she ultimately does not forgive, it will be just enough for me to express my regret and sorrow to her."

Kronos then began descending to the ground as a small hut came into view. Standing outside the hut was Minda. She was wearing the same outfit she wore when Morrigan visited her the first time. Her arms were crossed, her face showed no emotion as they landed in front of her.

"My love I have returned," Kronos said as he landed. He quickly got low to the ground, head bowed, and wings spread out on the ground. "I'm sorry for all that I have done to you and our family. Although it has taken aeons, please accept the humble apology of a foolish dragon."

"Forgiveness? Such an easy word to throw around," Minda sighed as she turned her back to Kronos and looked upward. "Through the stress, the struggle, the disappointment, the pain!" Kronos winced at each word she called off as if they were physically beating him further into the ground. "Then you left us. You left us out in the cold. How long did it even take you to realise we were gone? Probably *decades*!"

She then lowered her gaze to the ground and brought her hands up to her chest speaking in a softer tone. "Yet for all that, I can never say I felt your soul wane. You were doing what you enjoyed." She turned to face Kronos, "I left of my own volition, yet it is not me who you should apologise to." Minda then approached Kronos and put her hand on his snout. As she did, he opened his eyes and Morrigan could see a glow between them. "See, our souls never waned," she began to tear up. "I never doubted you'd come back. It was torturous without you, but my own guilt kept me from returning to you, and I'm glad you came back to apologise."

Kronos nuzzled Minda and she hugged him for a few moments before releasing him and turning towards Morrigan. "Our daughter, perhaps we should now be apologising to no one but you and your brother. One lost to the flames of war, the other lost to the whispers of the wind."

"My… brother?" Morrigan questioned, tilting her head a little to the side. "I… have a brother?"

"Yes, Ardivia."

"Ardivia? As in Ardivian Space?"

"The same one." Minda responded. "I thought perhaps you may have noticed him in your visions and made the connection." She then produced a small orb. Half was black; the second half had a grey, cloudy look to it. It had an unusual glow to it as Minda walked towards Morrigan, holding it out. "It would be faster to simply give you this."

"What is this that you didn't give to me when we first met?" Morrigan asked as she looked from the orb to Minda, to Verthandi and back to Minda again.

"When we first met you were still unstable. I instantly recognized you, but you did not know me. Had I given you this you might have suffered even more, or maybe even died. You were in no state to accept this, or any other information. I even contemplated not giving it to you, however, circumstances now require you to have it. Even if you don't trust anything we say, you will need this now more than ever." Minda grabbed Morrigan's wrist, shoving the orb into her hand.

As soon as it made contact with Morrigan's hand images began flashing through her mind. Dragons and humans living together, laughing, Kronos and Minda standing together getting a picture taken, Minda sighing as she stared out a window, and then the moment when Verthandi killed her. Her head felt heavy, and her legs felt like jelly, and her mouth opened, but no sound came out. The colour seeped out of the orb as Morrigan collapsed to the ground.

"Your diplomacy has failed, so it now falls to me to wash my hands with the blood of our persecutors," a voice boomed in Morrigan's head as the memory flashes disbursed. Her vision then slowly returned, and the pain slowly subsided. She sat up and for a brief instant thought she saw the silhouette of a man's figure before being blinded by a white light, finding herself back looking upwards to Minda. She looked at her arm, and from the elbow up it was now a slightly reddish-brown colour. When she ran her hand down her forearm, it felt a little rough instead of perfectly smooth. She also felt an itch on her back.

"Still irritated by your own wings," Minda said. "You never did like them or get used to them."

"Either way, she will need them now," Kronos interrupted. "Luna isn't about to let her just waltz around unchecked." There was a small pause before he continued, "Neither will Ardivia."

"But he's my brother, wouldn't he listen to reason from me?" Morrigan asked. "He could help against Luna and the others!"

"Maybe, yet the bigger question is, what has he been doing all this time? He did not come through the gate with me originally, nor does it appear he came through the gate with you."

"Still in Tumahab maybe?"

Minda bopped Morrigan on the head, "Hush child, I'm thinking aloud. I'm well aware of that, but the greater question is *where* in Tumahab. He couldn't be in any of the city centres otherwise, he'd be well aware of the events that recently transpired. Additionally, I can't say he had a particularly.... favourable... opinion on dragons."

Morrigan perked up and clapped, "Oh! I read a note from Ardivia Fae in a cave in Tumahab. Something about beware of Sol and Luna and that a 'we' was headed towards Asteria."

"The old capital?" Minda frowned.

"The current... capital." Verthandi corrected her. "The council moved the capital back there after they were fully established." She then paused, "But I have heard of no attacks or misgivings about the place. The move was brought forward by Luna as a means to recapture our former glory and tradition."

"But wasn't the reason it was moved in the first place because of ongoing tensions and the eventual rampage of my dear Kronos?" Minda interjected. "Didn't the magicks they use to contain him contaminate the area?"

Verthandi shrugged, "So they said, but there was no contamination when we visited the area before moving the capital back..." She paused for a moment, "Although there was an odd tingling sensation when we first got there, but it soon passed."

"And you never thought to question it?" Kronos said as he shook his head. "Guess they don't make them like they used to."

"Either way, we can assume he's not there anymore," Minda interrupted.

"How about Neo Asteria?"

"But we saw Neo Asteria get destroyed! They detected it when it phased into their side of the divide! What would have stopped the others from being found and destroyed?"

"What is this… Neo Asteria… you refer to?" Minda asked.

"It was a place where dragons and people were coexisting peacefully with each other. They thought we might have been tailed by the Rannsoknardomari, so they moved to the Tumahab side of the divide. When we switched, we were immediately detected by Luna who set about destroying the place."

"Sounds like an inside job," Kronos huffed. "And how do you know the town was destroyed?"

"Luna seemed pretty intent on destroying things. Luna's army was making quick work of the town's defenders…"

"Yet you managed to escape from what sounds like an almost instant detection," Kronos interrupted. He continued in a louder voice, "You two, alone survived. Why? Did you not stop to think about it?" Neither Verthandi nor Morrigan said anything, remaining silent with their heads hung low. Kronos then let out a large sigh before continuing, "Look I don't mean to be mean, but there are some things that need to be picked up on so that we can best approach this situation."

Chapter 19

"What a touching family reunion," a voice interrupted their conversation. They all looked up and saw Sol hovering above. Sol landed a short distance away, a broad smirk on its face. "But this will be the last happy scene you will have unless Kronos and Verthandi kill the human and is that... a Fae?" Sol added in utter disgust.

"You mean the ones controlling you and your actions?"

"Nonsense!" Sol roared. "The sentients have always needed our guidance. Tis why we kept the link with them. Now they claim to be our equal. Don't tell me you believe that rubbish as well." Sol paused for a moment before continuing, "Hmph, of course you do. Their stench and stupidity have rubbed off on you."

Without hesitation or warning, Sol spewed flames at the group. Kronos gathered Minda and evaded upward while Verthandi picked up Morrigan and did the same. As they made it above the flames, Sol was already above them shooting two fireballs; one at each dragon. The fireballs both hit their marks, sending the dragons crashing back to the ground. The impact caused them to drop Minda and Morrigan. All seemed dazed as Sol coiled to pounce on Minda, but as she was about to pounce, Kronos fired his breath weapon, forcing Sol to abandon her attack and fly up high into the sky.

Morrigan grabbed Minda, dragging her back closer to Kronos and Verthandi. Sol charged a giant fireball and launched it at the group. Kronos spread his wings around everyone to block the attack. The ball exploded on contact with the wings, disbursing heat and fire everywhere, knocking Kronos back. Sol landed back on the ground, flames oozing from her mouth. "And so, it all ends. None of you are fit to see the world born anew and will be purged."

"Stand down Sol!" a voice yelled out from behind Sol. Behind Sol stood two figures; one dressed in full body Rannsoknardomari armour, and another dressed in the general knight armour. Morrigan recognized them as Milotis and Charlie.

Sol laughed, "Milotis, your organisation has no more power. They are dead and you will be too if you think you can threaten me!"

"Our organisation may be dead, but we have sworn an oath to slay all dragons, and even if at one time you were one of us, we will uphold that oath!" Milotis yelled as he drew his weapon.

"Foolish Mortal!" Sol bellowed as he unleashed a breath of fire on the two combatants. Screams could be heard as the fire incinerated everything around it. Sol grinned once she was finished and turned again to face Kronos and his family.

"Seven hundred," a voice spoke through the crackle of the fire.

"What?" Sol's grin faded as she turned back to the smouldering ground behind her.

"Seven hundred years," the voice spoke again. The flames were suppressed, and the smoke and ash cleared, revealing Milotis still standing. The heavy armour started to crack and crumble as they continued. "Seven hundred years is a long time to wait for vengeance. I almost thought the time would never come." As the helmet crumbled away, it revealed a woman's face. Her eyes are as blue as the sky with short, blonde hair. Her tall and broad stature remained the same.

"The girl from Gelba," Sol sneered. "I seem to always miss one of you, don't I?"

The woman clasped her hands together and slowly opened them. A thin line of black energy formed between them until they were a little more than shoulder width apart and the line materialised into a blade. She grabbed the hilt with her right hand and pointed it towards Sol. "Their blood will flow until it sates our vengeance." Her blade and armour gave off an eerie bluish black hue as she stepped forward disappearing for a split second then reappearing behind Sol. "Until there is nothing left of their existence but an echo in song," she added, thrusting her blade into Sol's back.

"What *are* you?" Sol demanded as the sneer melted away from her face. "Only a chosen few have mastered that level of skill."

"A millennium of rage in a bottle," she said as she sheathed her blade. Sol burst into a ball of fire that lasted a few moments before burning itself out, leaving behind two wispy red orbs. The woman approached them, absorbing them into her hand. "I thought for a moment you were the Master Ardivia, but I was mistaken."

"You know where we can find Ardivia?" Morrigan asked. "Tell us where!" she demanded.

The woman turned to face them. "I do not know where they currently are, nor have I felt their energy for some time. Having spent a long time with the Rannsoknardomari, one did visit for a time, but suddenly those visits stopped, and I was unable to pursue their location."

"Then help us find him!" Morrigan interrupted.

"No," the woman said abruptly, looking away, as she turned to leave, "I must return to my fallen friends and give them closure. The ones from my village I have avenged, the ones in the Rannsoknardomari have yet to be fully avenged. I have no need to locate someone that doesn't want to be located." She looked towards her right where Charlie had stood, but now only a blackened crater remained. "Rest well friend, you have been avenged." She then turned away from the group and began to spread her wings.

"Mio? Katherine is still alive, maybe in the capital," Morrigan said as the woman prepared to take off.

"That is… comforting," she said as she hesitated for a moment. "They all survived that night…" she whispered to herself before adding in a more audible tone. "Thank you for that. We may yet be able to salvage things." She quickly flew off to the west before anyone could comment further.

Morrigan turned her attention back to her parents. Kronos was leaning up against some rocks and Minda was examining him, while Verthandi stood off to the side. He winced as she applied some ointment to his wounds.

"Sol had gotten stronger since we last sparred. I can only imagine Luna would be stronger," Kronos said as he rested his right arm and wing across his body letting Minda inspect them.

Morrigan was about to step towards them when a loud boom sound was heard. Everyone looked around to locate the source of the boom when they heard a second, louder boom.

"The sky!" Verthandi exclaimed as she pointed upward. A white edge preceded a purple hue that slowly moved across the sky. Slowly what looked like a mirror image of the world came into focus, spreading across the sky but maintained the purple hue.

"They're collapsing the space to join the two worlds," Minda remarked as she looked skyward.

"But wouldn't colliding two worlds kill everything including Luna?" Morrigan asked. "That accomplished nothing other than complete destruction."

"Except, the two worlds had to come from somewhere," Kronos interjected. "Worlds don't just explode from nothing after all. However, if I'm remembering astronomical data properly, the collision would wipe out everything, including both worlds, but the worlds would then be reborn as one."

"But that still will not help if everything dies!" Morrigan wailed.

"Then that means Luna obviously has a spot that will protect him and his hoard from the destruction." Minda climbed back down to the ground and Kronos stretched his wing to test her dressing. "It's good," he said, smiling briefly at his wife before returning back to their prior conversation. "I suggest we get to this Neo-Asteria. Its existence and demise seem quite suspect, and if Ardivia was heading to Asteria it might shed some light on his whereabouts."

"How do we know he wasn't killed when they moved the capital back?" Morrigan asked.

"We don't, that's why we check. Hypothesize, Test, Observe and Verify, then disprove or prove your hypothesis. That is how you learn things in life, so long as it doesn't kill you, then your life will serve as a warning to others."

"You won't find much there…" Morrigan sighed as she stretched her wings.

"That is for me to decide," Kronos growled as Minda got on his back.

. . . .

As they flew to where the cave was, they soared over charred land where the dragons had attacked. They heard screeches and roars in the distance but took care to avoid them. As Minda looked down at the charred landscape below her, she sang the following song in a slow, sombre tone:

Rannsoknardomari

Where have you gone?

The war you had taken can no longer be won

Dragons have come

Grounds burn like the sun

The sheen of your company

No longer shone

Nowhere to hide

Nowhere to run

A world once safe

Has been overcome.

Soon they reached the mountain where they had first met Itzl and Chimalli. Minda stopped singing as the group descended to land. As before it was cold on the approach when Kronos suddenly stopped and looked up.

"What's wrong?" Verthandi and Morrigan echoed as they turned to wait for Kronos.

"Do you not feel it?" he growled as he refocused his vision on Verthandi and Morrigan. "This place is of Tumahab origins."

Chapter 20

"But how can it be of Tumahab origins and not be in Tumahab?" Morrigan asked.

"Well, we travelled through; maybe this was a test object they sent through first?" Verthandi shrugged.

"No, I would recognize this aura anywhere," Kronos said as he reached out towards the mountain. "It's Beacon Tower, we designed it as a landmark that no matter what happened, we would be able to find ourselves." Kronos touched the mountainside and after a few moments of channelling, the snow and rocky look faded away to a tall obsidian spire.

"Wow, that's been here all this time?" Morrigan spoke wistfully as she looked up, almost bending over backwards as she tried to see the top.

"Come," Kronos motioned everyone through a doorway. "If this is here, there is something that I need to confirm." The group followed Kronos through the door. Inside the floor and walls were made with the blackest of obsidian, yet it had a gleam to it that made it appear brand new. There were not many carvings or markings on the wall, and everything seemed to be one long smooth edge. Not a sound was heard, except for the echo of footsteps. Kronos eventually entered a room that was pitch black except for a shimmering circle near the far side wall. Kronos approached the circle and saw it was almost a clear mirror. As he touched it, ripples formed on its surface.

Morrigan felt a sharp pain in her head and a resonance that seemed to mirror the ripples in the pool as she fell to her knees and her vision faded. When it returned, she was facing the winged person she had seen in a previous vision. The mirror behind him had stopped rippling and a dragon appeared at the door.

"Foul Fae, today you shall burn. You and your ilk!" the dragon hissed.

The Fae smirked and held out his right hand, "On the contrary my former allies. For my father has given me the tools to dispose of you." He opened his hand revealing a crystal.

The dragon at the door let out a laugh, "Foolish boy you would be killed as would we for using such a tool."

"And that is where you are wrong. For once, I am glad I'm not fully the same as you." The dragon at the door charged and devoured the man whole. However, a short time later the dragon began to reach, just before a light engulfed the room. As it faded, the man was standing, unharmed next to a glowing red wisp which was absorbed by the crystal. The man then morphed into the dragon he had just absorbed as more dragons appeared.

"Any sign of the traitors?" Luna barked.

"They have gone through the gate," he responded.

Luna grimaced and growled before turning to address the others outside the room, "Round up the remaining Faes and sentients. We shall show them the consequences of standing against us!" Luna and the others then left, leaving the one dragon in the room. It reverted back to the winged man.

"So how does the world look?" he asked as a shadow of similar shape formed behind him.

"It looks as it does now, but without the dragons," came the warped response.

"Excellent," the man smirked. Morrigan's vision then faded out and she returned to the dark room. Her head was in Minda's lap and Verthandi and Kronos stood around looking down at her.

"Good, you're back with us," Minda exhaled. "You collapsed and I was so worried!"

"I'm sorry mum," Morrigan groaned as she sat up and rubbed her head with her hands. "I saw a vision of something that happened here. Or at least the second part."

"Oh?" Minda said, rising to her feet then helped Morrigan to hers.

"Before I had seen this room, you left with another guy. He had wings, like mine. You were arguing over an orb, and he pushed you through what he called a gate. He then turned and I saw him get eaten by a dragon, but then burst out, and morphed into the dragon. The morph was good enough to fool Luna, but then he turned back to his normal self and started talking to a shadow. He said at the end that he had tools given to him by his father and he was glad he wasn't fully the same as the other dragons. I assume he was Ardivia."

"You would assume correct," Minda responded. "But who the shadow is, I don't know."

"It is also him," Kronos said as he returned to the pool. "I should be proud he has managed to take my work so much further, yet I am afraid for what he has done in exchange for it."

"What could he have done that is so bad?" Verthandi asked.

"Now I know for sure you two did not stumble onto a new Asteria. You probably stumbled into the old one." He then touched the pool, and it began to ripple. An image slowly began taking shape as Kronos continued. "These mirrors are gates. Time gates. That's why this tower is still here. That's why the dragons can feel a connection to the Terrakonans in this world. Both worlds are the same, just untold years apart."

"But I thought you stopped the time travel experiment! I thought you wanted a world free of the Seers!" Minda yelled at Kronos.

"I did, but I was obsessed with completing it. If we could go back in time and correct every mistake we made? Go back and save all our loved ones from their worst disasters."

"But what is life if it comes out all the same?" Morrigan interjected. "What good is life if you can orchestrate it exactly the way you want? We might not have been a split family, but would we have been a family at all if we could reverse things?"

Kronos smiled a little, "Your mother said the exact same thing, but I was determined. I didn't want to say I had started something and never finished it. So, I went back to it, but in hiding it from Minda, I cut her off. Then she left and I wanted more to complete it. To be able to tell myself what the mistakes were, to be able to save my family. But then Luna swooped in and destroyed everything. He was against anything that would allow sentients and dragons to coexist together. My last chance at redemption…. Gone. I lost it."

He sighed and looked at the mirror as the scene of a city started to come into focus through the ripples. The background of the city soon started shimmering red and finally the image of Kronos smashing through the buildings. "That was the scene that everyone always remembers. A dragon gone mad, rampaging through the countryside. The final piece Luna needed to banish everything." He then smashed his fist into the pool, disrupting the image and it faded from sight, "All I worked for destroyed. Luna has much to answer for."

There was a small silence before Morrigan spoke up, "So that painting we saw…"

"Was an image drawn up by this pool." He then looked at Morrigan, "However, I cannot explain your introduction to Chimalli and Itzl."

"Perhaps with the shapeshifting ability, Ardivia could have simply changed shape and introduced himself. Even if he spoke regularly, as has been shown before, she does not remember him," Minda interrupted. The pool water once again began to form an image as the ripples settled. This time the image was one of a cloudless day. The sun was shining bright and there appeared to be dragons and people doing activities in a park.

"That's the image we saw!" Morrigan gasped as the image clarified itself.

"That is… Asteria…" Kronos and Minda echoed each other. They looked at each other and then at Morrigan and Verthandi.

"What?" Morrigan demanded. "What is so wrong?"

"Could it be that you two relived a memory?" Minda thought aloud.

"Together?" Verthandi snorted. "And at the same time? It felt so real though."

"It's not unheard of," Kronos responded. "You two share everything, thoughts, actions, even dreams. The pool serves as a pool of memories; in it you two would have had similar ones. Even Morrigan if you don't physically remember Tumahab, you have walked the lands at one time." He paused and looked again at the pool as the image seemed to come to life with the people and dragons moving, the grass and trees swaying in the wind, and the babbling brook that flowed through the image. "Yes… perhaps Itzl was no more than Ardivia. Once he got you into the pool, the rest took care of itself."

"But why would he lead us somewhere and not reveal himself?" Morrigan demanded as she stomped next to the pool.

"For the same reason I didn't," Minda mused, crossing her arms then bringing her left hand up and tapped her on her cheek. She tilted her head to the side and looked at the image in the pool. "He was probably testing you. Both of you."

"Testing us for what?" Morrigan groaned.

"Luna is my guess," Minda shrugged.

"That… is not entirely true," a voice came from the entrance. Everyone turned in unison to see Nome walking towards them. She was walking slowly, clutching something close to her chest. Her eyes were bloodshot and there were water streaks down her cheeks.

"Nome! What happened?" Morrigan asked running over to meet her halfway.

"Morrigan get back!" Verthandi yelled. Morrigan stopped to look back as Nome smirked and exploded into a blast of energy. Verthandi jumped forward and blocked the blast with her wings.

"Impressive reflexes," a voice echoed. "At least one of you is paying attention this time." The voice faded into a maniacal laugh.

"Are you ok?" Verthandi asked Morrigan as she opened up her wings.

"Fine, I'm fine," Morrigan responded standing back up. "More importantly, who or what was that?"

"I... don't know..." Verthandi admitted as she looked at the spot where Nome exploded. "I know for sure it's not Nome, but the voice seems familiar... yet not..." She then turned to Kronos and Minda. "Do you two have any ideas?"

"No," Minda shook her head.

Kronos did not respond. He seemed engrossed in the pool which had now become muddled. His gaze seemed to not waver, nor did he seem to acknowledge the others calling out to him. Minda punched his arm and he jerked up.

"Oh, sorry I was just... lost in thought." He slowly turned to face Morrigan and Verthandi. "The voice you heard; I have not heard in a very long time." He shook his head, "In hindsight I should have seen it sooner..."

"Seen what?" Minda asked as the pool faded to black.

"Luna and Sol, sun and moon. Together they make an eclipse."

"Now I know where you're going with this, but no one has seen the Eclipse Dragon for *Aeons*," Verthandi interrupted as she moved towards Kronos. "We don't even know where he went."

"What are they talking about?" Morrigan asked Minda as she stood next to her mother with a furrowed brow and crossed arms.

"An Eclipse dragon," Minda shrugged. "I've never heard of such, which means it must be some old dragon lore."

"And if you're saying it's old, it must be ancient..." Morrigan remarked before feeling a sharp slap to the back of her head. "Ow! What was that for?" Morrigan yelped as she rubbed her head.

"Are you trying to call your mother... old?"

"Not at all," Morrigan responded with a nervous laugh.

"Good," Minda responded as she relaxed her stance. She then injected into Verthandi and Kronos' conversation, "But enough on that, what is an Eclipse Dragon?"

"Supposedly it is one of the four Heavenly Dragons along with Okeanis, Celeste, and Titania. They created the world and afterwards took their leave. Some say it was because they were exhausted, some said they fought amongst themselves."

"What do you believe?" Morrigan asked.

"They all died through infighting. That's what we were *all* told," Verthandi huffed.

"Yes..." Kronos' voice rumbled, "but..."

"Now is not the time to hesitate," Minda chimed in. "Don't you think your secrets have gotten you in enough trouble already?" She paused for a moment and looked at Kronos dead in the eye. "For once, the truth. All of it."

Kronos hung his head and took in a deep breath and let it back out slowly as the others gathered around him. Slowly he raised his head and spoke. "During my research, I had found that the Heavenly Dragons were all sealed away as they did not see a way that sentients and dragons could co-exist. In their absence, they established the Seers to maintain order and to prove the case that the sentients could be trusted. If they were wrong, they'd forever relinquish their power, but if they were right then they would erase everything and start things anew."

"This may seem like a stupid question, but how do you seal yourself away? Wouldn't you need something more powerful than yourself to accomplish that?" Morrigan raised her hand.

"Well, if you believe some of the legends and stories there is a Mother of Dragons. The story goes that they were laid to rest in her bosom, and she watches over them until the time is right for them to reawaken," Kronos responded. Then he added with a shrug, "But no description of such a dragon exists, so it's likely just an anecdote to make it easier for us to accept."

"That sounds highly uncharacteristic of a dragon," Minda remarked sarcastically. "I've always thought dragons were about the logical and not the whimsical."

"We are indeed," Kronos huffed. "But it was probably added for the sentients as they liked to ask a million questions and believe in the whimsical. Probably why it's nothing more than a fable and hearsay."

"Maybe..." Morrigan spoke slowly gazing at the ground, lost in thought. She then snapped her head back up to look at Kronos. "That said, is it likely these dragons would employ a scorched ground policy?"

"Very likely..." Kronos said in a daze before snapping his posture to face his daughter, "But what makes you say that?"

"I saw a vision when I was captured. The world was scorched and the smell of burnt bodies was heavy in the air and the sky was a purplish hue. The only person that was there was a woman dressed in pink. They claimed I was responsible for the destruction after handing over Nome to the Rannsoknardomari."

"Who is Nome that she would cause such a shift?"

"Katherine's sister," Morrigan responded without missing a beat.

"No, that is technically not correct," Verthandi spoke up, waving her claw.

"What do you mean?" Morrigan frowned and crossed her arms. "They seemed like sisters to me."

Verthandi chuckled before shaking her head, "No, they are mother and child. Katherine simply treats her as a sister because it was easier for Nome to grasp to the concept when she was younger that her mother simply didn't age." She then looked at Kronos and added in a graver tone, "Her father is Nogomain, or more correctly, High Dragon Nashmaw."

Minda gasped. Her mouth dropped open and when she looked over at Kronos she saw that he had an equally shocked expression on his face too. They both then looked at Verthandi.

"I take it that's a bad sign," Morrigan remarked.

"Very…" Kronos said once he regained control of his jaw. "No, Nashmaw you couldn't have," he said, shaking his head.

Chapter 21

"What's wrong?" Morrigan demanded.

Kronos heaved and let out a long sigh before facing the group. Although looking at the group, his gaze was far beyond them. "The Mother of Dragons story aside; we were told that Nashmaw was the key to reawakening the Heavenly Dragons. If he has a progeny, then that ability passes on to them. However, if they were to be killed, then the seal automatically releases itself. Considering the current state of things, the heavenly dragons would have no problem breaking everything back down to basics."

"Then all we need to do is find Nome," Morrigan said cheerfully with a clap, "and problem solved!" There was a pause and Morrigan's smile began to fade as Kronos' expression failed to change.

"It's not that simple," Kronos finally sighed. "Firstly, it's unlikely Nome herself knows as you don't just simply do and undo seals. She would need an absurd amount of energy, not to mention having to know exactly where to go." He then turned to gaze into the pool, "Yet there seems to be something sinister even with that. Faes were wiped out, we all personally saw to that, yet within the past day I have heard of or seen three; my own daughter, Nome and that mysterious person who duelled Sol."

"The girl who duelled Sol has a dragon crystal inside her," Morrigan spoke up. "She and Katherine both received them at the same time."

"Hmmm...." Kronos pursed his lips cupping his chin. "Even still, there is something else at play here. It's as if the Faes have some form of guardian or something that has interceded on their behalf. Perhaps this mother of Dragons story might warrant more looking into." He unfolded his arms beckoning towards Morrigan, "Come here my child, place just your fingers on the surface of the water, just enough that you feel the coolness on your tips."

Morrigan approached the pool and did as she was told. "Now close your eyes and clear your mind." She nodded at Kronos before taking a slow breath and closing her eyes. The water at first felt like it was still at her tips, but soon felt as if it was drawing her in, or at the very least she felt the water climbing up her hand and arm towards her torso. Feeling a little off balance Morrigan jerked backwards, holding her hand.

"What was that!" she screamed, rubbing her hand. "Did you not see me almost fall in?" She looked at Verthandi and Minda and they both shook their heads. Kronos motioned Verthandi over next to Morrigan.

"Ok, do that again, but this time Verthandi I need you to place your claws on Morrigan's shoulders."

"Alright," Verthandi nodded as she got behind Morrigan.

Kronos then spoke to Morrigan. "Clear your mind, don't be afraid. Verthandi is here with you, let the water flow. Verthandi has your back."

"O...k..." Morrigan responded with some hesitation.

"We can do this," Verthandi smiled at Morrigan. She then placed her claw on Morrigan's shoulder. "I got your back; you just look forward. We've got this together." Morrigan nodded and again placed her hands on the surface of the water.

She took a deep breath and closed her eyes. Once again, the water seemed to flow up her arm towards her torso. She felt as if she were losing her balance and falling in. The coolness of the water caused her to flinch, but she felt the warmth from Verthandi at her back. The gentle warmness overtook the cool of the water and allowed her to push past the liquid feeling of the water.

For a moment there was complete silence. The trickle of the water had disappeared, along with its coolness. The only sound she heard was her own breathing and heartbeat. Then she heard a voice. It was very faint at first, but gradually became louder to the point she could make out that the voice was calling out to her.

She opened her eyes and found herself floating in an empty darkness. She could see her own body, but as she looked around, she couldn't make out anything else. She tried to put her foot down on solid ground, but again there was nothing there.

"Who are you?" she demanded as she glanced around.

Upon asking, a ball of bluish-purple energy formed. The ball then morphed into a silhouette of a person with wings gradually extending out from the upper torso. Colour seeped in from the wingtips, starting as a dark blue before the tips became a pure white. The torso and legs then filled in with a shirt and shirt of the similar motif as the wings, blue with white edges. Finally, the head took shape and colour, first with blue hair, then brown skin and then two golden eyes.

The person called out again to her, but this time ran past her. As she turned, the darkness was gone, as the wings of the person seemed to colour the sky blue. She looked down at her feet and saw she was now standing in a large field of flowers. They were small white flowers with a yellow centre. The grass was green, and the sky was clear, not a single speck of white against the sheet of blue. The person stopped in the middle of the field, their wings now tucked away as they stopped and looked down at the ground.

"Of course this is where you are," the person chuckled. "Your parents want you back at the house; they say they have an important announcement."

"I'll be there in a minute," she heard her own voice respond as an arm rose up out of the flowers.

"Promise?" the person asked, a hint of depression in their voice.

"Promise!" her voice responded as she made a V with her pointer and middle fingers.

"Ok!" the person then spread their wings and flew back across her.

"You always did like flowers," the voice echoed as the scene faded away to darkness. "You'd spend entire years cultivating and nurturing them. You enjoyed their company, oftentimes more than you enjoyed the company of others. Yet even then, I was watching over you.

Morrigan heard a slight ring and turned around again. This time she found herself under the large marble dome in front of Verthandi who was flanked by Noctus to her left and Nogomain to her right. The shadows were long and Verthandi could not look her in the eye.

"I've seen this. This is when Verthandi killed the original me," Morrigan thought aloud.

"Or did she?" the voice echoed. "Turn around and face your doubts." She turned around and behind her was the hooded figure she had seen in a previous vision. However, this time she was up close and although the visage looked like her, it was not a female's face, but that of a male.

She was speechless as she heard the same exchange she had seen in a previous vision. However, this time as the blast whited out the view, she heard Kronos' voice. "If only we could reverse time and correct the mistakes we made. Then we could live as a happy family again." The light faded and this time it was the same place, but darker. A single beam of moonlight shone down into the hall. All the seats were empty, but Morrigan became aware of a nearby person crying behind her. She turned around to see a young girl collapsed on the ground crying.

"Why do you cry little one?" a voice asked.

"Because they killed my brother," the girl sobbed. "It was supposed to be me, but they switched us. And now I'll never be able to see him again."

"Now, that is simply not true," the voice echoed. "You are a keeper of time. Neither dragon nor human." There was a short pause before the voice continued, "If you wish, I can help you to see him again."

At this remark, the girl looked up and Morrigan could clearly see it was her. Her eyes were red from crying and her hair was dishevelled, but the features were that of her own. A pale arm extended into the moonlight, "Come. We can help to right these wrongs."

She wiped her tears away, "Really? We can?"

"Indeed, we can," the voice echoed. As her younger self stretched out her hand to touch the mysterious person, their face came more into focus.

"*Rion!*" she gasped as they touched, a blinding flash occurred before fading once again to the black nothingness. "What is the point of all this?" Morrigan demanded. "Who are you?" her voice echoed in the hollow darkness that surrounded her once more.

"Where are we?" the voice chuckled as the figure once again appeared before her. "We are in the endless sea of your mind and soul. I am merely showing you flashes of your past that might help you further down the road." The figure extended their hand to Morrigan. "Come, let us become whole again."

"And what if I don't?" Morrigan asked as she hesitated to extend her hand.

"Then you will be doomed to repeat the same mistakes for all eternity," the figure flashed a large smile.

Slowly Morrigan inched her hand forward, only stopping for a moment to see if the figure would move their hand. It didn't. She touched her fingertips on theirs and she felt a cold sensation seeping through her fingertips, causing her to flinch back.

"You don't have to do this if you're not ready," the figure said as the smile melted away. Morrigan looked at her hand. There were no signs of injury and again looked at the figure's hand still steadily waiting for her. She took a deep breath and without hesitation thrust out her hand forward.

"Welcome back," the person spoke as they locked hands with Morrigan. As they did Morrigan felt a sudden rush of energy that felt like it would blow her back before a light shone from behind the figure that engulfed first them and then her as if travelling out of a tunnel. "Finally, I can return to you that which I have kept for so long," Morrigan heard a voice echo as the hand she was holding dissipated into the light.

"Come back!" Morrigan yelled as she grasped for the hand that was no longer there. As she tried to reach out again, the light dissipated, and she found herself on the ground reaching up to the sky. Verthandi's worried face looking down at her.

"You're back!" Verthandi said softly. "We thought we'd lost you after you collapsed a short while ago," she said as she wiped away a tear.

"I saw... a light..." Morrigan murmured, slowly lowering her hand. She screamed out in pain as she felt a searing sensation go from her shoulder, along her arm to her hand. It went numb for a brief moment before the pain subsided. She looked at her arm and the marking had extended from just the wings to include a full body along her arm, and a closed eye on the back of her hand.

"It's as I thought," Kronos said as the water in the pool began to recede. "This place serves as a link between worlds." He looked towards Morrigan and Verthandi, "This pool held something for you two, although I cannot say what."

"She's... whole..." Verthandi replied. "Her markings are complete," she added as she gestured to the markings that now covered her entire arm and glowed a faint green.

"If being whole is this painful, I want to go back to being half," Morrigan groaned.

"No, this is better," Verthandi said softly as she touched Morrigan's forehead with her own. Morrigan felt a gentle pulsing of energy as Verthandi's aura seemed to sync with the aura of the markings. She raised her hands, placing them on the side of Verthandi's face. The pain subsided and was instead replaced by a warm, comforting feeling. She closed her eyes as she left the warmth and comfort overwhelm her.

"I promised you I'd find you and bring you back," Verthandi said as a faint green glow enveloped both her and Morrigan. "Now you can have access to your full powers," she whispered.

"Thank you for coming," Morrigan said with a warm smile as she was still enveloped in a green light. There was now an open eye marking on the back of her hand.

"The Eye of Ta'el has opened for you. May the path forward be made clear as the skies we soar," Verthandi grinned as the marking on Morrigan receded and disappeared into her arm.

As the light began to fade, the last bit of water in the pool began to gravitate towards each other into a glob. "And with that, you should no longer need my guidance," they heard a soft voice speak as the figure materialised. There were no distinguishing features to speak but the water formed a very elementary silhouette of a person.

"Ardivia!" Minda gasped, "Where are you? We've looked all over for you!"

"Or if not where, tell us what you are up to," Kronos growled as he stepped forward.

"I am up to nothing, though it would do you well to stand down Kronos, I am quite harmless in this form." The outline faded a little and the water began losing its form. "As you can see, I do not have much time left. Ardivia died centuries ago, and I have been but a keeper here. But, with Morrigan's memories and abilities restored, Ardivian Space will cease to exist. If you are to survive the onslaught Sol and Luna will bring, you must team up with one equal to them. Nogomain's spawn, Nome in the West. Only then will you be able to save that which you have worked so hard for."

"And what if we don't?" Kronos snapped.

"Then I will be greatly disappointed in you making the same mistakes as before," the voice said in a grim tone. The water then lost its form and dissipated into the air, and the room returned to its normal lighting and Morrigan fell to all fours, breathing heavily as her wings receded into her back and her eyes returned to their normal hue.

Chapter 22

"So Ardivia is dead," Kronos slumped. "All this way for nought…" There was a boom heard overhead.

"Snap out of it," Minda slapped Kronos. "I know our son is dead and you never got to speak with him, but he divulged information that would be able to help us prevent the total calamity that would otherwise befall us!"

Kronos raised his head and looked at Minda while she continued, "Your griping and moaning will only repeat the same mistakes if we sit here. Morrigan is nearly dying on the floor, having to bear the weight but she isn't letting it get to her. We're this far because we all pushed and never got hung up on what we couldn't do."

"Yeah dad we can mourn Ardivia… afterwards… but let's not let his sacrifice be in vain," Morrigan huffed as she struggled back to her feet. Verthandi gave Morrigan a shoulder to lean on as she started to catch her breath.

"You're… right," Kronos said as his posture picked up. "I'm… sorry… for this display. You are all working hard, and I too must do the same and not wallow in my own pool of self-pity. I died once for my work; I will not let it happen again."

"Good, now let us make haste to the West," Minda declared, pointing to the exit.

Once again, taking flight, Kronos carried Minda on his back, whilst Verthandi carried Morrigan on hers, with Kronos flying in Verthandi's tailwind. They did not have to fly long before they felt a gathering of energy.

"That almost feels like Nogomain's energy," Morrigan quipped as a treeless area appeared. Or rather, the area's trees had been ripped apart. Jagged stumps surrounded a lone figure in the centre. Looking more closely they she battered trunks formed a distant circle around thaw that the battered trees circled a figure. Upon closer examination they realised that the figure was in a squatting position, arms wrapped around it, hands moving up and down the opposing upper arm, a faint purple flow emanating from their body.

"Stay back!" Nome yelled as the group alighted near her. "You killed her..." she sobbed. "Why did we even help you?" She slowly stood up and turned to face the group. "Kat helped you... like she always does, yet you're here and she's not. Why did you just leave her there to die!" Nome screamed as she clenched her fists and tears began streaming down her face.

"We tried to help, but they insisted we move without them!" Morrigan responded. She hung her head and spoke in a quieter voice, "I'm sorry Kat and Nogomain died, but they did it so that we could live." She raised up her head to look at the seething Nome as she continued, "But we need to work together before--"

She was cut off as a dark bolt shot from Nome's hand across Morrigan's face. "No, we don't." Nome scowled. "All I've ever known, Kat, Nogomain, Arnhem... I can't hear them at all anymore. All I hear is the cries of death. And you death bringer, brought them." The aura around Nome began to expand, enlarging her wings. Her skin tightened into armoured scales, which spread to cover her wings. "If you wish my aid, then you'll have to prove to me that you're worthy of it!" Nome spread her wings, expelling a large amount of energy that would have blown Morrigan off her feet if Verthandi didn't shield her with her wing and stand at Morrigan's back. The stumps and broken trees that were not already at the edge of the clearing were blown back further into the woods.

"I've got you partner," Verthandi said as the energy wind died down and Nome focused her sights on them.

Nome folded back her wings, charging straight at Morrigan and Verthandi. Her speed was such that Morrigan lost sight of her momentarily, "Life coming at you too fast?" Nome jeered as she reappeared behind the duo and slashed an attack at Verthandi's flank as she dashed by. Yet it was Morrigan who screamed in agony, as she staggered to the right.

"What?" Verthandi was perplexed. She had been dealt the blow, but Morrigan felt it sharper than she did. Before she had time to recover, Nome had turned around and was closing back in again, unleashing a flurry of attacks that Verthandi did her best to block. Once again, she felt as if she defended well but Morrigan lowered her stance and began to breathe heavily. "What's going on?" Verthandi questioned aloud as Morrigan fell to one knee and leaned heavily on her right arm.

"And so it all ends, as it should have begun," Nome cackled as she held out an open hand, releasing several bolts of lightning that struck the ground around Verthandi and Morrigan before forming a cage. "You in a cage, except this time, there is no Kat to talk me down. So long, you won't be missed." She began to close her hand and the electric bars began to spin closer together. Her face illuminated by the electric bars, jaw clenched, eyes narrowed as Morrigan flinched from the burning bars.

"I'm sorry, I don't know what else to do," Verthandi whimpered before a fire ball blasted at Nome causing her to release the cage back to its original size as she was forced to block.

Verthandi looked at the source of the fireball and saw Kronos rearing for a second attack. Nome brought her wing in front of her to parry the second fireball. "That one stung a little," Nome scoffed, flexing her wing as one would flex their arm.

"I will not stand by as you destroy my daughter," he heaved before he felt his neck muscles tighten and he started gasping for air. He grabbed his neck and looked at Nome. Her aura was completely black, with the only distinguishable features being red eyes and the white of her grinning fangs.

"I have no qualms with you Kronos, actually I should thank you for this," Nome's voice began taking on a double tone. "Your work paid off in the end, it's just too bad you don't understand just how important it was."

Just as Kronos felt his head at its lightest and the world started to go dark, a thin blue beam pierced through the sky, aimed at Nome, she raised her wing to block, but it passed through undeflected, piercing through her left upper torso. Kronos fell to the ground gasping for air and the lightning cage dissipated as Nome's eyes dilated, her mouth opened in what looked like a gasp and her body fell limp on the beam before falling backwards along the beam's trajectory to the ground. As she fell, her wings receded back to their previous size and her skin returned to normal as the dark aura faded away.

From the sky descended a person with large blue webbed wings. "Now what," Minda muttered as Kronos struggled to catch his breath and Verthandi stood between the newcomer and Morrigan. As the person drew closer and alighted, Mio's features became visible. Her blue eyes seemed even more of a reflection of the sky, while her blonde hair now almost seemed white.

"Fear not, I have not come to bring further harm," she spoke as she held out her hand. "Only here to settle the madness." She looked towards Nome for a brief moment before turning towards Morrigan. "We were told Dragons and sentients once lived together. We were told that they were separated and lived on different worlds." She vertically held out her hand which pulsed in a blue light. "Different worlds yet a different time."

"They are! Tumahab is a parallel world in time and space. Separated by Ardivian Space. This has been proven!" Kronos wheezed.

"Hmph, parallel," Mio mused turning her hand inwards and looking at it. "Parallel lines do not intersect. Though I don't know what, this blue hue is the warmth of another. Another who arrived in my dreams shortly after the destruction of Mokey. It was distant at first, as if it was too weak to drag itself out of the depth of my soul. Yet I could feel its presence gradually creeping up, as if it wanted to consume me, but lacked that final push to do so. No matter how many times it crept up, I put it down only for it to return time and time again. This sinking feeling of loss that only seemed satiated when seeing Sol destroyed." She closed her eyes and lowered her head slightly, allowing her hand to rest on her chest. "I didn't fully understand until Gilbert's Madness. How he screamed late into the night, thrashing and convulsing as if under constant attack by an unseen foe. Temporarily, he would emerge victorious, only for darkness to swallow him again." She put her hand down and looked towards Kronos, "Did you not find it strange that Nome had a dragon to almost immediately bond to? You knew she was Katherine's daughter borne from Nogomain's seed, yet almost co-incidentally she had Arnhem waiting for her?"

She paused for a moment; her mouth contorted into a perturbed frown at Kronos' silence at the question. "Nome and Arnhem are the same entity. She was born on this side of the divide, Arnhem born on the other. Their abilities are one, and the reason they are often feared even among older dragons. But this is where the parallel ends. This is where the worlds collide. Upon death, Nogomain and Katherine's abilities pass on to their children. If they are parallel worlds, Nogomain's should disappear on its own, but they didn't. They transferred to an overwhelmed Nome. And it was that unexpected power you saw brought to bear just now."

"That's an odd case!" Kronos roared. "You bear no proof of your hypothesis."

"Oh, but I do," Mio said with a wicked smirk. "As does Gilbert and your very own daughter." Before anything else was said, she pointed a finger at Verthandi and shot a blue beam through her upper left torso. As had happened during the Nome fight, Morrigan clutched her chest and fell to the ground.

"Stop! What are you doing?" Verthandi cried.

"Verthandi, you died aeons ago. As did all the Seers during the revolt. Your essence lives on in Morrigan through the Fae Crystal. It is not you who projects on Morrigan, but Morrigan who projects. You are an accumulation of her old memories."

"That's not true!" Morrigan fired back. "She breathes and lives as do I. She has helped me this far and we'll be together to the end."

"Have it your way," Mio sighed before shooting a blue beam through Verthandi's head, causing her to fall backwards and land on the ground with a thud in a supine position.

"I feel strange…" Verthandi shivered. "I must have hit my head harder than I thought…"

"You're picking a terrible time to make a joke," Morrigan remarked, kneeling down next to Verthandi. "You can get back up and we'll prove Mio wrong."

Verthandi tried to heave herself up but was unable to move. "No, I can't move. It feels numb…"

"Come on, stop playing…" Morrigan said before she felt her own hand pass through Verthandi's claw. "Your claw!" Morrigan gasped. "What did you do!" Morrigan cried. She looked to Mio whose face remained emotionless. "Don't worry, we'll think of something," Morrigan cried as she turned again to face Verthandi.

"I'm not sure we can avoid this one," Verthandi said weakly. Her body had become more translucent, seeming to be gathering in small green sparkles of light across her body. It was hard to tell if she was crying or if the sparkles were the green light, "I've been searching for you, but maybe it was you who called out to me."

"No! You're not going anywhere!" Morrigan cried as she tried to clutch onto some part of Verthandi. "You can't disappear! Not after all we've been through! I still need you to teach me how to use my abilities properly!"

"I guess this is goodbye. I'm sorry for being such a disappointment," Verthandi said as she raised a claw up to Morrigan's face to wipe away her tears. But the tear went right through her claw and continued to stream down Morrigan's face. "Time is short, and you have places to go."

"No! Don't leave me!" Morrigan cried as Verthandi's body faded from view, only leaving the pale green outline before it too dissipated. Morrigan continued sobbing before slowly getting to her feet and facing Mio. "You *killed* her!" she shrieked. "She had done no wrong to you, yet you killed her!" There was an up-welling of energy, and a green aura began to surround Morrigan. She then let out a scream and the gathered energy exploded away from her. As most of the vegetation had already been cleared by Nome, Morrigan's expulsion whipped up clouds of dust and debris. Khronos shielded Minda from the dust with his wings. As the dust settled, they heard a low growl and saw two pale green eyes peering through the cloud of darkness.

"And there you have it, the merge is complete," Mio cackled as the dust cleared and Morrigan came back into view. Or rather it was Morrigan, but with the appearance of Verthandi. She let out a roar as she unfurled her wings fully and batted away the remaining dust. "Behold Verthandi in her full Seer glory once more!" Mio announced before showing a toothy smile, her eyes began glowing a deeper blue. "Now let us see if this child is better than the last. Come Dragon of Time, let us see if you have learned from your mistakes," Mio said as she transformed into a large white dragon.

"Okeanos? No, it can't be," Kronos grunted as he recovered from the energy blast. "You should be sealed with the others."

"What should we do?" Minda clutched unto Kronos. "Is there no way to resolve this without violence? There has to be a way," she cried.

"This is one thing she has to do herself," Kronos said as the two dragons grappled with each other before ascending to the sky. He watched the skies as the two combatants danced across it, "They are both too powerful for us, and if we interfere, we might not make it back out as Morrigan is in a blind rage."

Minda's face was perplexed as she looked up to Kronos. She shook her head, wiped some tears from her face and yelled, "Morrigan, come back to us!"

Chapter 23

It was dark when Morrigan opened her eyes. She looked around and saw nothing other than her own body. The deathly silence was punctuated by a primal roar. She struggled to her feet as she tried to locate the sound, but it had once again gone quiet. She walked a few paces, whilst craning her neck and straining to hear any sound.

"Morrigan...." she heard a dismembered voice whisper. "Morrigan...."

"Who's there?" she demanded as she stopped walking and listened. However, no answer was forthcoming. She started to walk again and she heard the voice speak again, "Morrigan... Morrigan..." She paused once more in the darkness and this time she heard a soft sobbing.

"Verthandi?" Morrigan thought aloud as she strained her eyes through the darkness. Soon Verthandi's silhouette came into view. Her head was hanging low as she was standing opposite another dark silhouette. Neither acknowledged Morrigan's arrival.

"You're a useless Dragon, only useful as a cog for the mechanisation of the mighty!" the hazy figure spoke. "You bring nothing but death and destruction, only your blood proved useful to us!"

"No, that's not true!" Morrigan yelled, running forward. The two disappeared as she got within strike range and once again the area returned to its empty blackness. "Where am I?" Morrigan asked before feeling a thump that reverberated in her chest causing her to fall to one knee. She clutched her chest to ease the pain but felt heavier. A ripple formed on the ground and out of the ground in front of her and a shadowy figure emerged standing over her.

"There is a saying, those who are afraid of making mistakes, often make the mistakes they are trying to avoid. Because they are trying to avoid the mistake, they never acknowledge it has been made and therefore never learn from it," the figure spoke with crossed arms and in a harsh tone. "All you have ever done is run away. From Gelba, from Nome, from Asteria. You are quickly running out of space to run, yet instead of learning, you simply repeat the same mistake until you have nowhere to run. By then, it is already too late. You have failed where you tried so hard not to. Do you wish to continue the cycle? This cycle of perpetual running as the world crumbles around you?"

"No," Morrigan sulked. A single tear ran down her cheek and to the ground below her. She hugged herself as the tears began to stream more freely. "Have I become that which I was afraid of happening the most simply by avoiding the problem? Or was Charlie right in saying all Terrakonans become raging beasts in the world?" As it rippled, she felt herself begin to sink into the void. "All I wanted to do was live a peaceful life with my friends and newfound family. I don't know how to be a dragon, and neither did I want anyone to die for me. I just wanted to be an example of peace and kindness."

"Morrigan!" she heard the hollow echo in her head again. "You're not alone! You don't need to do this by yourself anymore."

Who is that? Morrigan thought. The voice sounded familiar yet distant. Does it really matter what the voice is? All I've ever done is bring pain and suffering to those who have helped me. She recalled all that had happened over the past few weeks. Katherine, Nome, her own parents... Even if the sound she had heard was a voice trying to reach her, it was probably going to do no more than condemn her for her failures. That's all she was after all... a failure. The darkened figure disappeared into the darkness leaving a hollow, echoing laugh as Morrigan sank deeper into the mire.

"Morrigan, you better not lose or I'm going to blast you in this life and the next one!" she heard Nome's voice yell out. "You won't get off so easily for wasting my food and my time!"

"Nome?" Morrigan said in a daze before she heard another voice.

"You can't save everyone, but you'll never know if you don't try. No matter the odds, if you believe in yourself, you can live without regrets," Morrigan heard the soft echo of Katherine's voice.

"Not everyone is a believer of your beliefs, all you can do is change the world one sentient at a time," Chimalli's voice echoed. "Even my own children leave me, but they always come back, sometimes with friends. If you can't believe it, then who will?"

Morrigan's head snapped up at the end of the sentence. She grits her teeth, grimacing, "Yes, Katherine, Nome, Asteria, they all fought for what they wanted. Even if they were at odds with me and each other, they still held onto their beliefs. Verthandi too would not want me to give up, she'd want me to carry on until she got back."

Slivers of light began to permeate the cracks in the floor beneath Morgan. "Yeah, Verthandi wouldn't want me to give up. Just like with the Rannsoknardomari, she came back once the drugs wore off. She put her life on the line to save me from their trial. Even though I blamed her for being selfish, she stuck through." The lines of light grew thicker as she remembered Verthandi.

"Verthandi, come help me!" she yelled out as the darkness shattered. Morrigan felt an upwelling of air and the area was flooded with light. She fell through the floor and started plummeting towards a green field below. She closed her eyes and crossed her arms above her head to cushion the impact of landing. Instead of a hard impact on the ground, she landed on a cushion of air that slowed her to almost a complete stop allowing her to land on the ground prone with nothing more than a soft thud.

She looked around and found herself in a field of flowers. The very same ones she had growing in her hometown. She knelt down and felt the soft petals, lined with some dew. A gentle breeze blew as a shadow formed over her.

"Verthandi?" tears streamed down Morrigan's face as she looked up at her friend's familiar face. "Verthandi! You're back!" Morrigan cried running over to hug Verthandi. Verthandi flashed a grin and reciprocated the hug allowing Morrigan to cry into her torso. "I thought you left me alone and losing you was my final failure in life."

"No, never," Verthandi responded, "Remember I said the exact same thing when we first met? You didn't leave me back then, and after all that, what good would I be if I didn't return the same faith?" Verthandi held Morrigan aloft, using her left claw to wipe away Morrigan's tears, cradling her face with her right claw so that she looked towards Verthandi.

"But how?" Morrigan cried. "Wait, isn't this where we first met? In Ardivian Space?"

There was a bolt of lightning followed by a dark orb descended from the sky to the ground. It remained static for a moment before morphing into the shape of a person. The last thing that formed was the face, which caused both Morrigan and Verthandi to gasp. There standing before them was an exact doppelganger of Morrigan, except she was oozing dark energies.

"Ardivian Space never existed, at least not in the capacity that you believe it did," Shadow Morrigan smirked. "Instead of it being a continuous area, it was constricted. Only to the two souls that called out to each other and synchronised. That is why it is coloured in accordance with the wants and desires of the two inhabitants." Shadow Morrigan then knelt down and touched one of the flowers, causing it to wither and die. "Yet even here, there are separating forces. You seek the path of perfection. Always wanting to be the perfect angel to everyone, whilst you banished me, your passion, your anger, your despair to a corner and tried to suppress me. But now, as your body rages, I have been released and come to claim this body. But in order to do that I need to first suppress my opposite as she once suppressed me. I will extinguish your flames of hope once and for all and take both your body and dragon for myself. Taking with it the hope and light of your world." The skies began to darken. Clouds formed as the world began to grow a little dark and a strong wind picked up.

"You're wrong!" Morrigan yelled as she leaned into the wind, clenching her fist as she fully turned to her shadow self. "Yes, I admit I've been afraid of taking action, and pretended that I had been better for not wielding my power. But Verthandi has been with me through it all. Verthandi has those same fears. Fears of us being separated and fears of never being worthwhile to anyone else again. But we've stuck together through it all, and that's what makes us partners!" She glanced back at Verthandi, "We are there to support each other and though we each have our differences, we come out stronger than we go in."

"All talk," the doppelganger smirked as she formed a dark sphere in her hand touching down on the ground, causing the grass in the area where her feet landed to wither and die. "Let us see whose mind is truly stronger, your light of hope or my void of despair."

Verthandi shot a fireball and hit the doppelganger in the chest causing it to take a step back. Morrigan too recoiled back as if punched in the chest. She clutched her chest and grimaced, falling to one knee.

The doppelganger made no attempt at dodging Verthandi's attacks, but Morrigan kept shuddering and yelped in pain every time Verthandi tried to attack. Was the doppelganger moving so fast that it was beyond their sensory capabilities? Morrigan winced as she felt another sharp pain in her chest before she yelled out, "Verthandi stop!"

Verthandi's maw was open over the doppelganger as Morrigan issued the order, ready to crunch down. Instead, she drew back and looked towards Morrigan who was struggling to get back to her feet. "Why hesitate? She would kill you without a second thought," Verthandi growled.

"But she hasn't. She hasn't even moved from her spot. No, I understand now," Morrigan coughed. "We are all the same, you me and her," she added as she dragged herself next to Verthandi. "It's why I was hurting when Nome was hitting you, just as I still hurt as you hit her." Morrigan took another step towards the doppelganger. "We all have our dark sides and I'm no different. Thoughts and fears that we lock away from everyone and pretend don't exist." She reached out to the doppelganger who simply nodded its head and sighed.

"So, this is your answer?" it responded as its shoulders dropped and hands hung limp on its side.

"You are as much a part of us as we are of you," Morrigan declared. "To kill you is to kill us. Everyone only likes to acknowledge the good in them, but few ever acknowledge the dark. Perhaps if more acknowledged the dark, then we would be more accepting of the darkness in others and be able to see them capable of light as well."

"If this is your choice, I will abide by it," the doppelganger raised its hand to meet Morrigan's. "But if you ever tire of playing in the light, I'll always be waiting to take over the reins."

"I know," Morrigan nodded as their fingers touched. The shadow doppelganger melted into Morrigan, and light returned to her surroundings until all that was left was a ball of purple energy in her hand which she then clutched close to her. "Wherever there is light, there is also shadow. Both are two parts of the whole and dismissal of one is the death of the other. Together as one we fight!"

A light emanated from Morrigan as her sight returned to the battle at hand. Her opponent seemingly put their wing across their face to avoid being blinded by the bright light. Morrigan let out a loud roar that shook the ground spreading her wings, her entire body glowed green, gathering energy into a large orb above her.

"I see, so this is why my mistress has such interest in you," Mio thought to herself as she lowered her wing. "But let us see if you're truly able to wield that power or if you are still lacking!" She charged Morrigan, but found herself frozen in mid-air, unable to move forward, as if a hand had grasped her and was holding her in place. She felt her body being compressed; bones cracking could be heard as she howled in pain before the force that had stopped her caused her to move backward towards the ground.

Though Mio landed on her feet, she found herself unable to move her limbs and fell to the ground. She looked up above her, towards Morrigan, who had her arms extended above her head with a large green orb of energy between them. She closed her eyes smiling, "Yes, I think they're in good hands now." There was a small pause before Mio opened her eyes back up again. "Funny, I thought losing may have been harder, but it almost feels welcome. Nearly one thousand years of anger and pain brought to an end by one of my own." By now the energy had finished charging and Morrigan hurled it towards Mio. She made no attempt to block it. Only a smile and a whisper, "See you soon old friends," as she was engulfed by the ball of green energy. All that was left was a crater where Mio once was.

As the dust cleared, Morrigan heaved a few times, before reverting back to her human form. Her breathing was still laboured as she fell forward on the ground. Kronos and Minda rushed over to her side. She knelt down rolling her face up to cradle her head so she could put her hand near Morrigan's mouth. "She's exhausted," Minda said as she felt Morrigan's breathing which had a slight quiver to it. "We need to get her and Nome back to the hut so we can rejuvenate them. They will need all their strength for the upcoming confrontation."

Kronos nodded. He gathered Morrigan in his arms and then helped Minda to put Nome on his back before they flew off from the clearing, back to Minda's hut. As they lifted off, smoke could be seen in the distance, and the roar of dragons echoing all through the air.

Chapter 24

Morrigan woke up some time later. It was quiet, save a gentle breeze blowing through a nearby window. She grimaced as she felt pain in her right arm as she tried to prop herself up. She was back in Minda's hut but scanning the room she saw no one. "Mom... dad...? Are you there?" she called out. But no answer was forthcoming. She got out of bed and slowly moved over to the window and gasped at what she saw. The sky was a red colour, as she had seen in her premonition back at the outpost, she shook her head in disbelief. She closed her eyes and opened them again, hoping that it was a trick of the light, that maybe her sight was not adjusting after waking up. But the red sky still remained when she opened them. "But why?"

"All you bring is death and destruction," a voice spoke from behind her. She turned around to see Nome standing in the doorway, lips set in a scowl, eyes still as piercing as the time they first met, arms crossed while she began to walk towards Morrigan. "Maybe if Kat had let me kill you from the start, she'd be here now instead of you." She unfolded her arms, and held out her right hand, and formed a ball of electricity. "Even your parents may have still been alive if it wasn't for you. You're a Harbinger of Death is what you are."

The words hit Morrigan hard as her mind scrambled to process what Nome had just told her. "My parents are dead...?" she stammered.

"As dead at Kat and Nogomain, and it's all your fault!" Nome said as she thrust her hand with the electric orb forward, straight towards Morrigan's face in one swift movement. The electric ball stopped so close to Morrigan's face that she could feel the static from it, jumping towards her face, crackling and sizzling. "I should kill you where you stand, another to the body count. To rid the world of such a deadly being." Morrigan felt the ball moving away from her, slowly before falling away completely as Nome fell to the ground on her knees. "But you're the only one left. If you go, I will have nothing. We're the last ones," she cried in almost a whisper.

"What! Are you sure?" she said as she knelt down and put her hands on Nome's shoulders.

"Can you not feel it?" Nome sniffled. "There is nothing left out there but us."

Morrigan backed away from Nome slowly standing back up. She noticed the lack of birds singing, the wind was not cool, and she felt a sense of emptiness and encroaching doom. Placing her right hand on her chest, she closed her eyes and exhaled. "Verthandi, where are you?" She tried to search inwardly, but the dragon did not respond. Has everyone truly left her? Had she actually killed off all those close to her? She looked down at the still sobbing Nome. The only one she had left.

She was about to reach out to Nome, when the sound of glass shattering was heard, followed by a roar that shook the building. Morrigan snapped her head back and turned to look outside the window. Descending from the sky was the same black dragon she had seen when she first met Verthandi.

"Ah, such a terrible oversight on my part," it said, unleashing a ball of black energy over the building. Morrigan put up her arms to block her face from the flying debris taking a step back to brace herself against the explosive force. As the dust settled, she slowly lowered her arms, the black dragon had now alighted completely on the ground and was facing her and Nome who had by now scrambled to her feet. Its face contorted into a wicked grin, golden eyes fixed forward. "You were wise to escape me for so long. How your parents hid you is a wonder all on its own, but now that I have you, you shall not escape me."

Morrigan morphed into her dragon form and charged the black dragon. It met Morrigan's front claws with its own, being pushed back as it tried to dig in its heels to stop Morrigan's momentum. Just as they came to a stop, Morrigan's mouth began to flame, and it pushed off from her, narrowly evading to the left as Morrigan spewed her breath weapon. It tried to form another orb, before Morrigan finished, but found his energy snuffed out.

"I have no qualm with you Seer, for one mightier than me is coming to expunge your stain off this world. I have only come for the youngster," it said as it pointed towards Nome.

"Like I would hand her over to you," Morrigan seethed. "You, like the rest, are simply afraid of what can be done if we work together and would instead tear us all down instead of building up!" Morrigan said before taking flight to attack the black dragon. "You killed my village; I am not about to let you kill something else that's of value to me."

It raised its claws preparing for another blast when a bolt of lightning sparked between them, causing them both to flinch and shield their eyes.

"No, it is you who shall not be going anywhere," Nome said in a snide tone as she formed her lightning cage around the dragon. "You threaten me, and I will respond in kind. Whilst I appreciate Morrigan's defence, I will not sit idly by and let you take anymore life, least of all mine." She held up her right hand and began closing it, which in turn caused the cage to shrink around the black dragon. "Now join those you so happily sent to the depths; depths as dark as your scales."

"Amateur skills from an amateur Terrakonan," the dragon huffed. Nome attempted to close her hand, but her hand would not close into a fist. She grimaced before gritting her teeth, using her second hand to apply more force to the cage. Yet as she applied more pressure, the dragon simply smirked. "Now it's my turn," it said as it started forcing Nome's hand back open with its wings. Nome tried using both her hands to keep the cage shut.

"You will *not* win!" she yelled defiantly mustering every ounce of strength before being forced into the ground as her energy was forced open and the lightning disbursed. She cradled her now limp right hand close against her torso.

"I take it back, you are definitely the prodigy of a dragon, but your powers are still severely lacking," the dragon said as the faint smell of burnt scales could be detected. "But ultimately, as I said, too weak." It held out its claw to enclose Nome in a ball, but Morrigan lunged and clamped down on its arm making it howl in pain. It attempted to grab Morrigan, but she released his arm and evaded the attack, flittering backwards to create some space between them again.

"I told you, you will not take the last of what I have left," Morrigan growled. "Even if you have no quarrel with me, in attacking Nome you are attacking me, and I will defend what little I have left with my all."

"Such determination will avail you not," he growled. "But to continue this fight would be foolish." He stomped the ground with his hind foot before quickly producing a brilliant flash that Morrigan had to shield her eyes.

"No, stop! Get away!" Morrigan heard Nome shriek. She fired a shot off in the general direction she heard the scream but strained to listen for any other sound as she waited for her eyesight to return to normal. Once it did, there was no sign of the dragon nor Nome. Morrigan crumbled to the ground as she reverted back to her human form.

"They're gone, they're all gone!" she sobbed. "Is it my destiny just to be alone in this world and everything around me dies?" She sat there crying, until she remembered what her father had told her, that Nome most likely did not know what she was capable of. "There... might be still time," she wiped away her tears. "But I have no idea where to start looking," she sniffled. She shivered as a chill ran down her spine before she slowly got to her feet. She looked at her hands, opening them wide before closing them into a fist and returning them back to an open palm. "Maybe it's just time for another leap, like at the Rannsoknardomari Trial." She extended her arms fully as she spread out her wings. "I might not be as knowledgeable as the rest, but this time it's up to me to not be a passenger and be a driver."

As she took off flight, she scanned the horizon, noting that there was not much to see other than forest below. The sky was still a purple hue, but clouds were beginning to form and with them came a stream of lightning which seemed to augment the purple to a darker shade.

Chapter 25

As she flew alone through the skies, searching for any sign of life, she all of a sudden understood the reason for the Travelin song. Comfort, one could say as she improvised her own, to keep her mind at ease, despite the circumstances she found herself in. She recalled the one she heard while in Asteria, Kronos' Lament. Perhaps, it was as her father had searched for her mother, so too was she in search of Nome as the only one she knew to be still alive.

Find me still searching.

For the one who saved me.

Searching still seeking

To quench the flame inside me

Promise to survive

Until we are united once more

Fire Eternal

Burning Infernal

Gone are the days so joyful

Even with work they're mournful

And so I fly waiting for that day

O happy day

When we can enjoy the twilight

Of a blissful silent night.

She changed some of the words to the tune, but it still served to pass the time in flight keeping her motivated that she will find something at the end. Just as Kronos had found her, she too hoped for the happy ending of finding Nome.

The green of the forest gave way to a brown barren wasteland. As far as the eye could see. There was no vegetation on the ground, only death. Dead people and dragons strewn across the ground with their weapons. The stench hitting Morrigan all at once, blood mixed with burning flesh of dragon and sentient alike.

The ground also bore scorch marks where flames had once raged. "It's just like I saw in my vision… Death everywhere. But I've just lost Nome. Am I to wonder for a week? No, because they said they had already reaped my soul. I'm already doing better than my vision, but if that vision was not of the future, why has it altered without me seeing it rewritten?"

Her thoughts were interrupted as she sensed something to her right. A gathering of energy? It certainly wasn't a natural gathering, so she lowered her altitude to avoid possible detection veering towards the direction of what she sensed. As she flew, a large obsidian tower appeared, jutting out of the otherwise desolate landscape. "This is the clue I need," she said to herself, increasing her speed to get to the tower base as quickly as she could.

She alighted at the base of the tower and found no sign of life, only the force of gathering energy. The base of the tower was very open, she could see straight through to the other side even though the sides were solid black. She was unfamiliar with the materials the tower was made of and upon closer inspection found it to have an eerie purplish glow to it. She circled the tower to make sure she had not missed any openings further up the structure. Finding none, she returned her attention back to the only obvious opening into the tower at the base. As she entered the tunnel, the only other opening in the black walls was an opening on her right. An opening about the size of a doorway that upon closer inspection she could see steps going upward.

"Guess it's only the stairs," she muttered as she approached the lone doorway. "You'd think with flying that dragons would appreciate not having stairs," she added as she entered the doorway. Looking upwards, she followed the seemingly endless spiral of stairs to the top. As she did, she noticed the hole in the middle of the spiral, "Maybe I *can* fly," she said, placing herself in the eye of it.

Spreading her wings, she began her ascent. Her wings barely missed the edges of the staircase, and it soon became exhausting to generate the lift required to fly straight up without any left or right motion or air currents. By the time she reached the top she took a moment to lean heavily on her legs to wait for her heavy breathing to return to normal. Once it did, and her shoulders didn't feel so stiff, she continued on through the doorway.

Nothing, not even the faintest of aromas could be detected. It was simply an empty room with nothing of note other than sliding doors that had two buttons next to it. The top button had an up arrow while the bottom one had a down arrow. "Why would this have a down arrow? I don't recall seeing any matching doors at the ground entrance," she thought aloud as she stopped in front of the door to ponder the buttons. "Unless it's an underground entrance," she pursed her lips and scratched her head. "If this is like Beacon Tower, would that also have counted as underground since it was in a mountain, and we needed a cave to reach it?" She thought for a moment longer before slowly reaching out and pressing the down button. After all, if this was a dragon tower, surely there would be nothing higher as it only got narrower and larger dragons would probably easily puncture if anything was further up.

The doors slid open. The compartment inside was large enough to fit a couple of people, but definitely not a dragon. She walked into the metal box and contemplated who or what would be waiting for her. This was clearly not designed for dragons, but she had not seen any other people alive since waking up at her mother's hamlet. She crossed her arms as the container moved downwards. None of the rooms thus far had been large enough for dragons, but Terrakonans could easily fit in them. Was this a Terrakonans Tower? Was this the Terrakonan answer to the Beacon Tower?

As the container came to a stop, she took a stance to spring forward if something were outside the doors when they opened. Much to her surprise there was no one at the door to greet her. She relaxed a little as she peeked her head out of the doors. To her left were another set of doors labelled 'Test Area'. To her right was a wall with a bench, though no one currently occupied it. Directly across was another door labelled 'kitchen'.

As the door closed behind her, the doors to the Test Area opened and a person walked out, fully covered from head to toe with some type of yellow outfit and mask. In their hands was a clipboard and a pen. "Welcome Miss Bloom," they spoke as they approached her. "I've been waiting for you to arrive. You've come for Nome, yes?"

Morrigan gasped and took a step back, "How do you know my name?" she demanded.

"When you get to be old like me, you know a great many things. I even know that you're trying to figure out if this is the same as your vision."

Morrigan was unable to see anything about the person beneath the mask and baggy yellow covering. She grit her teeth struggling to figure out how this person knew her so well but she had no clue on who it possibly could be. "Who are you?"

"Don't worry about that," the person chortled. They opened the doors they had just come through and beckoned for Morrigan to come. "Don't worry, it's safe. After all, we can't have the guest of honour have a bad experience. It would bode ill for us."

Morrigan cautiously approached the doors. She looked over the person, but still could not see anything beyond their covering. As she came alongside the person who was still holding the door open, she looked inside the room. Several others dressed like the person at the door were inside running experiments at several lab benches that she could see. She looked at the person holding the door for her. They nodded, ushering Morrigan in. The people already in the room made no motion or even acknowledged her entering the room and continued on with whatever they were working on.

"We are allies," the person spoke. "This is a transportation tower. It will send you across the divide and to Tumahab. You want to rescue Nome, and the only way of doing so is to stop Luna's plan on home soil. Once they gather sufficient energy from the local area, you will be able to cross over and get what you seek." The person walked over to a clear part of the bench and picked a large crystal that was sitting there.

The crystal was orange with a hexagonal shaped central shaft that tapered into pyramidal like points at the top and bottom. It was slightly larger than the person's hand as they picked it up. "Is that... a dragon stone?" Morrigan asked as they handed the crystal over towards her.

"Yes, because you may need one where you're going," the person responded.

"To capture a dragon. Do you think Luna and the Eclipse dragon will be that strong?" Morrigan looked at where the person's eyes probably were, lips pursed and brow furrowed, before looking back at the stone.

"I have no doubt," the person responded with a small pause before continuing. "Not that I doubt your strength, but this is extra insurance just in case," they added as they closed Morrigan's hands around the crystal. "It's made of a special citrine to increase your chances should you need to use it."

"I'll do my best," Morrigan nodded. "I'll defeat Luna and bring back Nome!" Her eyes began to water, "Yeah, the last of us. And bring happiness to this dying world."

"Good. If you've not got anything else, we should go up to the transport point," they said as they pointed upwards. "You're on limited time. Shed your tears now and shape them to strengthen your resolve." The person then walked back to the door and opened it again. "Come let us depart," they beckoned Morrigan. Morrigan nodded and quickly made her way through the door. The person pressed the up button on the wall and the doors slid open, once again revealing the metal box. The two got in and Morrigan once again looked at the person as they began their ascent.

"Who are you really?" she asked.

"Just a friend," they responded as they continued looking forward. "Do not worry about such trivialities as my name, just know that I am here to help you succeed because if you succeed, we all do."

"I see..." Morrigan looked at the ground a moment before refocusing back on the person. "But it's hard to believe someone you can't see."

"You had never seen Tumahab, yet you believed in it," the person responded without missing a beat. "Sometimes, you just have to have faith in the other person. That's how friendships are made are they not? You do not know a person, but you put your faith and trust in them and slowly it leads to something greater than either of you ever imagined. Two strangers making the impossible possible."

"If you put it like that," Morrigan groaned. "I guess it makes sense..."

The ascent stopped and the doors opened. This time there was a small room with what looked like a cylindrical portal on the ground. Wires and tubes ran from it along the ground to a console at the far side of the room. There were no windows or any other outward facing openings and there didn't seem to be any other doors entering the room.

"This device will teleport you directly to where Luna is. I suggest once you get there quickly get your bearings and move to where you feel Luna or Nome's energy. Probably Luna's as he's unlikely to be keeping it in check believing himself to have already won."

"Thank you," Morrigan said. She moved towards the portal and once standing on it, took in a deep breath and closed her eyes. Her mind wandered back towards that original vision she had.

'One week ago, you delivered Nome to the Rannsoknardomari. They made a public spectacle of her execution, sending her sister into a soul shattering fury. With the souls of Arnhem and Nogomain the Heavenly Dragons were able to open the gate between Tumahab and Terra. Dragons, sensing their time had come to exact vengeance for their separation from their beloved Terrakonans for so long poured through the gate. The resulting fight is the carnage you see before you'

Wait, this order is wrong. I thought they were delivering Nome when she was back in the library. That never happened, but the dragons coming through and the sky, and smell are all still the same. Furthermore, isn't Katherine already dead? Nome has already had her soul shattering experience but all of that happened after the sky changed. What... am I missing?

"Good luck!" came the call which disrupted her thoughts. The person waved to her as they punched in some commands. "May we be victorious!"

"Mhmm," she nodded haphazardly as the portal activated and the room was engulfed in a brilliant light. As the light faded, she found herself in a stone room that she instantly recognized. "This is the Rannsoknardomari HQ in Garlot!" She looked to her right and saw a bed with the window behind her. This wasn't just the same building, but it was the same room. Either this was a sick co-incidence or something more sinister was going on.

Meanwhile, back at the tower, the person at the controls to the portal laughed as they removed their hood revealing themselves to be Charlie. "By your hand will the collection be complete and then we shall have the power to create the world in our image," he smirked. By now the others who had been working in the laboratory had come up and were exiting the elevator, but their hoods were now off revealing them as Katherine, Minda, Mio, Solara and Gilbert. Their eyes were as blank and expressionless as their faces. "Thank you all for your hard work, I'll be taking your crystals, you'll not be needing them anymore."

Chapter 26

Morrigan easily felt Luna's power. Almost like a lighthouse in the darkness. But she had been warned he'd likely be flaunting his power. "Move forward and don't look back," she psyched herself up. She pulled out the crystal and it was pulsating a brighter shade of orange. Was it reacting to the environment? They had said it was made of special citrine. Perhaps it was preparing itself to absorb Luna. Her mind was still racing as she ran through the corridors towards Luna's power source when a thought hit her. Nogomain was black, and it's likely that's the crystal she had seen Katherine absorb in her vision. The other girl was likely Mio, who had become Okeanus and was blue. She had never seen an unused dragon stone, but this one she had was orange. Nome liked orange. Was she carrying her friend's dragon stone? But to what purpose?

She came to a stop and took the crystal back out of her pocket and looked it over. It was still pulsating bright orange. Was it really Nome inside? Or Arnhem? Her thought was interrupted by nearby clapping.

"I did not expect you to figure it out so soon. Perhaps I underestimated you, which seems to have been a frequent occurrence during this whole journey," Morrigan snapped up to see Charlie walking towards her doing a slow, sarcastic clap.

"Charlie! Why?" she took a step back.

"I've been watching you from the very beginning," Charlie said as he put his hand over his face and slid it down, revealing a new face.

"*Rion*!?" Morrigan stared in disbelief.

"Yes, it's me," Rion sneered. "As inheritor of Luna's Dragon Stone, I was ever privy to the happenings of the Dragon Council. But then it occurred to me that the Tumahab and Rannsoknardomari Council had the same name. Curious, I learned that Sol was already present and had begun to distribute stones for this day. A day when the dragons would believe their hour of victory would be at hand. Luna had made no small secret that I would be discarded at the first available opportunity, and so I worked with him, but also figured a way to usurp his power. I tried to get you as an ally, but you seemed ever content to coexist. And so it is, you with the final stone I need to complete the ritual to end this world and banish those conceited dragons back to books and wild imaginations."

"But what about us Terrakonans? Surely, we'd still miss our friends and partners?"

"I see you're still as naive and innocent as when we talked here before," he shook his head. "Not that it matters, soon you'll just be a distant memory as well."

"Not if I destroy the crystal first!" Morrigan raised her hand but was stopped as she felt a sudden thud in her chest. Her eyes dilated, jaw hung open and she clutched her chest as the welling up of pain started to overwhelm her. She dropped the orange crystal as she dropped to her knees.

"Thank you, I'll be taking that," Rion smirked, retrieving the orange crystal. "I'll also be taking this one," he sneered as he made a pulling motion and yanked one out of Morrigan, causing her to fall backwards in a supine position. "Speechless? I know, I have that effect on people," he laughed. "As a parting gift, I'll let you in on a secret. There is an old tale concerning the creation of the world. It was said to be created by someone only known as Mother of Dragons and Other Oddities. I would have ignored it if only Nome hadn't been intrigued by the same story that time we found her in the library." He stood back up, admiring both crystals he had in his possession, a wide grin spreading across his face. "I suppose a thank you is in order, even if you did let Nome originally escape from us, you have still brought her back to me."

"No, it can't end like this!" Morrigan thought she spoke, but no words came out of her mouth, only the stuttering of a person near death's door. "Verthandi, mother, father, someone... help me?" As her world began to fade, much to her surprise she saw a glint of orange. Was she... seeing things in her death throws?

"You really *are* hopeless," she heard a familiar voice before a warm aura was felt and her hair began to stand on edge. Slowly, she felt her energy return, her chest pain began to wane, and her vision stabilised.

"Nome... but how?" she said as she sat up and looked at Nome who was still crouched next to her.

Nome got back up to her feet, "Because Kat said it was the only way. They leaked the power out of the stones so that we can retain some of our Terrakonan abilities, but we're not able to fully transform into a full dragon anymore." She sighed as she looked down the hallway and then back to Morrigan with a frown, "I still dislike that you're here and she's not, but you have at least tried to defend me, clumsy as some of it was. Hopefully this gamble pays off and we can get them back..." her voice trailed off and she held the nape of her shirt.

"Don't worry, we'll get them back," Morrigan got to her feet and hugged Nome. "It'll be alright, I promise. I won't be a deadweight and we'll make sure Kat and the other's sacrifices won't be in vain." She felt a wet spot form as Nome rubbed her face into her chest before standing back up and away from Morrigan.

"Yes, let's finish this once and for all," Nome rubbed her eyes and nodded with a weak smile.

The two continued down the hallway and came to the room that was oozing Luna's energy. Nome prepared a lightning orb in her hand and nodded to Morrigan to open the door.

What awaited them in the room was Rion standing at the head of a table, his hands raised above his head, but his back was to them. The room was poorly lit, but beyond him appeared a faintly illuminated purple square and above him a circular light cloud had begun to swirl. "Oh, you two are full of surprises today aren't you?" Rion sneered. "But alas you're too late. Now watch as your world comes to an end and mine begins!"

"Oh no you don't!" Nome hurled her lightning at Rion only for Katherine to appear and block the spell. "Kat? Why?" Nome demanded.

"Because what better way to stall a child than to have their mother mete out some parental discipline," Rion laughed as Minda too appeared next to Katherine. Their hollow eyes seemed even more eerie in the low light. "Don't bother talking to them, they can't hear you. They are nothing but soulless dolls at this point."

"How *dare* you!" Morrigan seethed as she clenched her fist and formed an energy ball of her own.

"All this talk and no action, you'll need to be quicker than that if you aim to stop me," Rion laughed. Minda formed a sword and engaged Morrigan, whilst Katherine threw her own spells at Nome. Nome put up a shield to deflect the shots, but they bounced in all directions, some nearly hitting Morrigan as she struggled to dodge Minda's flurry of attacks. The deflection did have the advantage of also disrupting Minda's attacks who had to pull back to avoid getting hit.

"Close range it is," Nome said as she formed a lightning blade with her fingers. She rushed Katherine but found Minda parrying her attack as Katherine raised her hand to prepare another magic spell but was forced into defending as Morrigan unleashed a flurry of energy shots at her.

"Yes, continue fighting, it'll bring the end closer faster," Rion laughed maniacally. Minda then pushed Nome off her weapon before quickly following up with what seemed like a void blast. Morrigan shielded Nome who was still in the process of landing on her feet from being knocked back.

"Nome we're going to get only one shot at this. I'll distract them while you do your best to get past that barrier and stop Rion," Morrigan spoke as Nome retreated to be next to Morrigan. Nome nodded her acknowledgement to the plan. Morrigan spread her wings and arms and they began to glow with a faint green hue. "I've learned a few tricks too since we last met Rion, and here's one of them," Morrigan smirked as she brought her hands back together and clasped them. A ticking sound was heard before Morrigan added, "Nome go! Now!"

Nome didn't need a second invitation as she rushed in at full speed thrusting her blade into the barrier. At first, she was concerned about a counterattack from Katherine and Minda, however, both appeared to be still where they stood before. Unmoved as Nome impacted the barrier. At first, it appeared the barrier would hold, and Nome brought her second hand to pierce the same spot her first had landed. As she heard a crackling sound, she smirked as and applied more pressure, before seeing the cracks appear and the barrier breaking apart like a glass box. "I've got you now!" Nome took a step forward to lunge and attack Rion.

"You're too late!" Rion grinned as a blinding light shone through the cloud above him. Nome followed through with her attack as she became blinded by the light, a howl from Rion as the blade met with some resistance was enough to assure her that she had found her mark. As the light faded, they found themselves on a stone platform surrounded by black. As if the room they had been in had been cut from the world and placed in nothingness. The shadow corpses of Katherine and Minda also disappeared.

"Children, why have you summoned me?" a voice echoed. They all looked around to find the source of the voice as stars began appearing around the platform.

"I have come to request that the dragons be removed from this world! They and their ilk are a hurdle to the peace and tranquillity that us humans desire and long for!" Rion yelled into the darkness.

"A peculiar request to be sure," the voice spoke as some of the stars began to merge above the platform. They took the vague shape of a person before the light began to take a physical form as it was filled in by colour as they continued their descent onto the platform. A woman with light brown skin, short cut black hair with golden tips and was in the standard anatomical position. She wore a long white robe with navy blue trim. Embroidered around the base of the robe were depictions of dragons and people holding hands. The robe was held together by a navy-blue sash that was tied in a very neat bow in the front. A matching pair of light blue sandals adorned her feet, with her nails coloured in a similar tone. A few outside stars aligned to give her the appearance of wings, though as she descended, the outline did not. Her feet touched the ground without stirring even a speck of dust, her eyes finally opened to reveal their golden hue, which seemed to be accentuated by other golden specks, like freckles along her upper cheeks.

"I am Aerianna Xelha. Mother of Dragons. I have answered your call as you have undone the Seal of the Ancients," the woman's voice was stern, and cold. "So tell me, have the dragons and humans learned from their past mistakes?"

"No, they have not Aerianna, there continues to be fighting, so grant my wish and restore the world to one without dragons. One where humans can rule free of the influence and dangers of dragons and their ilk!" Rion yelled out.

Aerianna looked down at Rion a moment who was holding his injured side which was now soaked in red. "Allow me to heal your wounds so that you may be able to move again," she spoke as she knelt down to Rion's side.

As she reached out towards Rion, he produced a Dragon Stone and held it up against her face, "Your powers are now mine!" He laughed triumphantly for a few moments before Aerianna frowned at him. "Wait, why isn't it working! You should be in my thralls as your energy seeps into the stone!"

"Foolish boy, like so many before you. Though I am called the Dragon Mother, I am not a dragon." Rion howled as he felt a sharp pain in his side. Aerianna had a smug grin on her face as he looked down to see his chest impaled by a staff.

"I brought you here! You shouldn't be able to kill me," Rion wheezed.

"Even a child may kill given the right motivation," Aerianna spoke as she withdrew her staff and stood back up. She held her right hand up as it started to glow, illuminating only one side of her face. A perturbed scowl spread across her lips as she spoke, "I act on what's best for my children. That you believe me incapable of violence, or any form of self-defence means you make a mockery of what it truly feels like to have the wellbeing of others on your mind. You may have requested a favour, but it was borne out of your own selfish desires that you so abhor in others. As such you will not live to see the world you so desire."

"Curse you dragon!" Rion yelled as he became engulfed in light. His voice echoed as he turned to dust.

"You're not going to actually follow through with the destruction, are you?" Nome asked.

"At this point I have to," Aerianna responded without looking at Nome. She planted her staff into the ground, and it began to glow a faint white colour. Her voice was no longer sharp as it was when dealing with Rion but had returned to a more gentler tone similar to when she first arrived. "It has become far too unstable and if I don't destroy it now, it will eventually be destroyed."

"But surely there must be a way!" Morrigan yelled.

"And what? Watch it fall apart while the rest of you guys fight it out causing strife whilst blaming everyone but yourselves?" Aerianna fired back. She turned to face them; a scowl was now on her face. "Unless you can find a way to change my mind, this world and all that remains will become nothing but a distant memory."

"Not if we can help it!" Nome yelled as she took the few steps needed to close the gap between her and Aerianna. At the last possible second Aerianna grabbed her staff and side stepped the attack. She attempted a vertical slash, but Nome kept up her momentum to roll out of the way.

"You've chosen death!" she thundered. "Of course, you've chosen death," Aerianna sighed in a quieter voice, her face showing a momentary look of sadness as she echoed her first statement. She slid her hand down her face and took in a deep breath as she held her staff along her right arm and pointed it towards Nome, "Then show me your convictions, that I might change my mind."

Chapter 27

"It's two versus one, even if you are an almighty entity, the numbers are not in your favour!" Nome bellowed. "Think you can do that freeze trick again? Even if she has the best reflexes, if we remove them, then we win!" Morrigan heard Nome's voice echo in her head.

"Of course, I can," Morrigan nodded with a grin.

"Good," Nome grinned as she prepared to charge in again. As Nome flew in, she heard the tick-tock once and Aerianna's eyes froze, partially open, left foot taking a step back, both arms pulled back a little as if preparing a defence. "I got you now!" Nome pulled back her arm to prepare a punch. However, just as Nome got within touching distance, Aerianna's expression changed as a confident smirk flashed across her face.

"Surprise!" Aerianna said as Nome made contact with a full force ice wall that winded her, knocking her back a few metres. "Very nice try, I almost forgot for a moment I was dealing with a time dragon," she smirked. "But time stops for no one here. It always moves on, whether we like it or not."

Morrigan ran over to Nome, though kept an eye on Aerianna, who seemed content for the moment not to move from her current spot. "Are you alright?" she asked as she helped Nome back to her feet.

"Fine, a little woozy, that blast or whatever I hit felt like hitting the ground when I used to practise my divebombs," she shook her head. "But if individual attacks don't work, we'll have to double team her. She can't block both of us at the same time. You take the left and I take the right? Don't worry, my speed hasn't changed that much from a blow like this."

Morrigan nodded acknowledgement of the plan and prepared to rush her left flank while Nome attacked her right. They both hit almost in unison, forcing Aerianna to dodge upwards.

"So you guys *are* capable of teamwork," her tone had softened a little as she formed a double ring beneath her. "But remember that counter attacks are also part of combat." She grinned as she hit them both with a big fire spell. However, her grin faded to an open mouth as they leapt through the fire to follow up their attacks one on each flank still. "Use your elements to shield yourselves and then propel forward," she muttered as she gathered just enough of her wits to teleport a safe distance away from the duo. A smile crept along Aerianna's face as she faced the duo and they landed back on the ground.

"What's so funny? It's only a matter of time before we get our breakthrough!" Nome yelled defiantly as she and Morrigan landed back on the ground.

"I'd agree with you one hundred percent," Aerianna said as she brought her wings close to her chest and rested over her arms that had formed an 'X'. "But that would imply I always cede the initiative to you."

"Won't matter if we always take it first!" Nome yelled as she fired off a lightning spell, or it would have fired off, but as she was still before her and Morrigan quickly followed it up with a combined melee attack.

"Check. Mate," Aerianna grinned as she threw open her wings and arms, releasing a wave of pure light which shocked and stunned Morrigan and Nome. They flew back from the attack like leaves caught in a storm. Morrigan took the hit hardest as her world started spinning and she collapsed right on the ground. She tried to keep her eyes open, but they soon closed, and the sound of spells and weapons clashing faded into a distant echo.

She opened them a short time later. "Am I... dead?" she spoke aloud. She looked around and saw Verthandi nearby. She rushed to her feet and ran over to hug Verthandi. "You're still here! Then I guess I must be dead," she added as she looked towards the ground and her voice trailed off.

"No, you're not quite dead yet," Verthandi shook her head. "I told you, until the arches claim us, we remain forever as one."

"I could use you right now though," Morrigan sulked. "I could use a dragon."

"But you are a dragon," Verthandi chided her. "Kronos is your father, you're part dragon! Have you forgotten your pedigree already?"

"No, I remember," Morrigan said as she sat down and sulked looking at the ground. "But I'm nowhere near as strong as a dragon. Me and Nome are getting the smackdown of our lives from Aerianna. Every time we think of a new plan, she counters it with almost a single action." Verthandi chuckled, causing Morrigan to snap up her head and glare at her. "What's so funny? We're all going to be *erased* if we don't do something soon!"

Verthandi closed her eyes and smiled, "Aerianna. That's her name. A name I have not heard in a very long time." She looked back upon Morrigan's concerned face, "But what is her title?"

"Mother of all Dragons. But she isn't even a dragon!" Morrigan wailed as she put her hands on her head.

"You worry about the wrong part of the name. She may not be a dragon, but more importantly, she's a mother. Her spells hurt the more malice you bear towards her. If you, someone with dragon blood coursing through your veins bore her no malice. If you simply clear your mind and not see her as an enemy, but as a fellow living thing, her spells have no effect on you."

"What? That's the dumbest thing I've ever heard!" Morrigan yelled.

"You say that, but is she not here because there is eternal conflict? Was her first question not one of attack, but of if harmony had been achieved? Like us before you, in that desolate future, you lose holding on to what you think is the most logical answer and as a result the world dies. It's likely that we saw our own demise, due to not heeding towards that which may have been illogical or unheard of at the time. Aerianna is an illogical variable. She's called a Mother of Dragons despite never being a dragon. Perhaps, this is a sign, that in order to win, we need not rely on the dragon's strength, but their resolve, and that illogical thing you sentients refer to as emotions." Verthandi looked off into the distance, "Your time is up. You have to decide for yourself then which path to follow. Until next time."

Morrigan's vision faded once more and she became aware that she was breathing in dust, which caused her to sneeze and slowly push herself off the ground.

"Welcome back," Aerianna frowned. "I thought you had bitten the dust already, but your friend here has put up quite a spirited attack in your absence. Perhaps you can make it up to her."

Morrigan stood up straight. Of course, Aerianna would provoke her. But Verthandi was right. Thinking through this logically had gotten them nowhere. In the end, Aerianna clearly held the strength advantage, meaning there was only death that awaited them. If that was going to happen regardless, then perhaps Verthandi's approach wouldn't matter. Morrigan cleared her mind and kept her head down to avoid her eyes from seeing Aerianna's. She walked towards her very slowly.

"Are you *crazy!*" she heard Nome yell.

"Quiet Nome!" she fired back. "I promised you I'd try everything to get us back safely from here and I'm going to do all in my power to do so. She continued her steady march towards Aerianna and started thinking about her experiences since starting this journey. Katherine treated Nome with kindness and was soft until provoked. Then she became a vengeful being, unleashing an attack which killed everyone except her because she was not seen as an enemy, but a friend. Yet even before that, Katherine knew how to speak in a way that made Nome flinch, which as far as she could tell was not an easy task. Her own mother had left Kronos to find a better life for her. Even though she initially pretended not to know, it was out of care and compassion so that she would not interfere with the growing and maturing of her child. It all made sense...

Aerianna smirked, "You'll just be a sitting duck walking like that." She raised her staff and prepared to fire another fireball at Morrigan when she looked up.

"I understand now. You want nothing more than a safe place for your children," Morrigan said with a weak smile. "If we see you as an enemy, then you will unleash your fury upon us in order to protect that which you hold dear. But if we harbour no ill will towards you, your attacks have no effect."

Aerianna pursed her lips and for the first time since the battle had started, there was hesitation on her part to go on the offensive. The spell remained charged, but she did not launch it. "Though I guess since we're half dragons that makes you more grandma to us," Morrigan said before Aerianna shrieked and launched what seemed to be a large explosive supernova spell. The spell sent out a large shockwave, flattening what little debris was still standing and engulfing Morrigan in flames that even Nome felt at a distance. The dust slowly cleared, a crater in the ground where the spell had hit and in the centre of that circle Morrigan lay prone on the ground.

"Tch, teach you to call me grandma," Aerianna sneered as she prepared to turn back and refocus on Nome who was struggling back to her feet. However, Nome gasped as she saw Morrigan standing back up. Other than dust, Nome could not see any blood or injuries on Morrigan that weren't there before the attack.

"I get it. Verthandi was right. No matter the strength of your spell, it's amplified by your target's malice. If we see you as an enemy, then you will see us as an enemy. But by the same token, if we see you as one of the same, as a family, spells that can be used to destroy worlds have no effect, because the last thing a mother wants is harm to come to her child." She lifted her head and smiled at Aerianna, "Does this suffice for you? Or do I need to keep walking towards you and survive more spells?"

Aerianna's features softened and she smiled as her staff dissipated. "No, you have the right of it. I will not harass you any further. So tell me Morrigan, what is your desire for this world?"

Morrigan gasped and recoiled back at the mention of her name, "How do you know my name?"

"Your friend referred to you as such," Aerianna chuckled. "But more importantly, this isn't your first time here. You've been here before." Aerianna paused as she looked up to the stars in the sky. "Almost all those stars above us are different instances you've been here. Where you fought to the death because you had misguided yourself into believing that inaction was no action." She then brought her gaze back down to Morrigan, "You always had the conviction, but you had failed to understand it is not the pen or the sword that is mighty, but the hand that knows when to wield them at the right times. And so every time you lost, I used your powers as the Time Dragon to rewind the past few weeks, to give you a chance at reaching what you so desperately sought."

"Why not just explain it to us?" Morrigan asked.

Aerianna chortled, "Ophelia says the same thing. But I find that lessons are learned better when you have the learn with a few knocks to the head. After all, as they say no pain no gain," she smiled and lightly punched the right side of her head. "Of course, you had few memories of the reset week, so I had to guide you in a few places. Your visions of the bleak future were poorly assembled memories after your losses. Ophelia would make sure you were stable enough to return back before we reset, and that is why you always saw her at the end. Likewise, Ardivia had died centuries ago at the hands of Verthandi. Every time you saw him, there were times I could communicate with you to make sure you stayed the course and learned of different things that would help you make the right choice."

"I don't understand though, why go through all this trouble? Why not just let it end the first time?" Morrigan asked, her brow furrowed in perplexity.

Aerianna took in a deep breath and closed her eyes for a moment. She opened them and looked up at the stars. "I once sacrificed myself to save the world, do you think it would bring me joy to destroy it? If there was even the slimmest chance that one could save it, would you not want to save it?" Aerianna paused to take in a deep breath and momentarily close her eyes before locking her eyes with Morrigan's. "But then I met you. You who seemed determined to save the world, and so I peered closer into what would drive someone to save a world they hadn't cared much about a couple of weeks back." She then looked away, folded her arms and pursed her lips for a moment before continuing in a softer tone, "And when I looked in, I saw a younger me. You were not driven by greed or fame. You were driven by the desire to live harmoniously with your newfound family and friends." She then turned her head to once again fully be looking at Morrigan and Nome. "And so, I gave you the opportunity to prove yourself, and see if you could learn how to balance your strengths and your emotions. Follow your heart and desires but take advice and information from those close to you to solve problems. Something, even I had problems with." A weak smile formed across her face as she continued, "But then I met Ophelia and she taught me that sometimes both are needed. It's a fine balance you learn, but it's also the most fulfilling. Though I am still prone to outbursts, it's where some people said I had a dragon's spirit within me."

"So you're… really not a dragon?" Nome huffed as her posture dropped.

"No, not at all, but I have cared for several dragons in my time, and they in return treated me like a mother. And so, upon their return, the Legend of the Dragon Mother was born. However, the Dragon Council and by proxy the Rannsoknardomari both decided that having a story that involved a non-dragon caring for dragons was against their beliefs and fabricated the elemental dragon story. The longer they kept dragons and non-dragons apart, the more time Rion and Noctus had to put their plans into effect." A gentle wind chime sound reverberated through the area, causing Aerianna to take a step back. "Well, it appears our time together is up. For one final time, I will reset the past few weeks. But the world will be the way you imagine it."

"Will we ever see you again?" Morrigan asked.

"Probably not, but you never know," Aerianna smiled weakly, "humans get jumpy when they see magical things." She bowed her head and clasped her hands close to her chest forming a small orb of radiant light. "Goodbye my children, I hope you two have a peaceful and happy life."

The orb flashed and whited out the entire area, forcing Nome and Morrigan to shield their eyes. They felt the wind blow by, and the sound of a clock ticking as Morrigan felt her body moving away from where it currently stood.

As the light faded, Morrigan became aware of birds singing, a babbling brook and a blacksmith was hammering away at his latest orders. The smell of freshly baked goods in the air was giving way to the stench of manure as the sun was finally starting to clear the hilltops and shining down into a valley. She was lying in a field of flowers, her pail and a small shovel nearby. She sat up, and rubbed her forehead as she looked at the ground and groaned, "Was that all a dream?"

"Hey sis are you alright?" a voice called out as she felt herself being poked in the arm. Standing next to her was a man, slightly taller than her. He had red hair and was of a light complexion, wearing a green shirt with black trousers.

"Are you…?" she started to say before she felt a slap to her back and a familiar cackle as she turned around to see Nome, a wide grin on her face.

"Did you make another Cheesy pun that your sister just ignored you again, Ardivia?" Nome laughed.

"No, nothing like that. I just found her here with a mile long stare," he hastily responded as he shook his hands and head. "I was out here to get her for dinner before mother gets out here."

"Mother...? Ardivia...?" Morrigan echoed as she looked at the two standing over her in disbelief.

"Oh come *on*, you've seen us all early this morning..." Ardivia started to say before Nome cut him off.

"Perhaps she just had a bad dream or something while she was out here napping," she said with a nervous grin. "You know how she gets sometimes."

"True..." Ardivia mused before he turned to head back into the village. "Either way, be quick, mother will have dinner out shortly and you know how she likes us to be washed up and on time."

"I'll be right there," Morrigan said with a smile as Ardivia disappeared back into the village. Her smile melted and she turned to face Nome. "Is... this all... real?"

Nome slapped her, causing her to recoil and rub her cheek. "As real as that slap felt," Nome beamed. She then added quietly with a smile still on her face, "I guess, I should thank you for all this. Kat and everyone is still alive. We've all been friends for years."

"So... I have my family for real now...?" Morrigan's eyes began to water. Despite her cheek still stinging a bit, she felt her heart begin to swell.

Nome nodded, "All well and accounted for."

Morrigan hugged Nome and buried her face on her shoulder. Nome felt the tears beginning to soak her shirt and tried to push her off. "I'm sorry... I shouldn't be so sad, but these tears won't stop," Morrigan sniffled.

"It's... ok..." Nome whispered as she embraced Morrigan. "I feel the same, but it certainly is good to have everything back to normal."

Morrigan nodded through her tears as the two ended their embrace. She looked up to the sky as it began changing from blue to red. A lone star shone in the sky. "Thank you," Morrigan whispered as she looked upon the star before looking back in front of her and returning home.

www.ingramcontent.com/pod-product-compliance
Lightning Source LLC
Chambersburg PA
CBHW071516170626
46811CB00007B/2869